TINDER

SOULLESS KINGS MC

ANDI RHODES

NICOLE CYPHER

Copyright © 2020 by Andi Rhodes and Nicole Cypher

All rights reserved.

No part of this book may be reproduced in any form or by any electronic or mechanical means, including information storage and retrieval systems, without written permission from the author, except for the use of brief quotations in a book review.

Cover Artwork - © Amanda Walker PA & Design Services

This one is for all of our readers! Because of you, we get to do what we love every single day. We can't thank you enough for that <3

ALSO BY ANDI RHODES

Broken Rebel Brotherhood

Broken Souls

Broken Innocence

Broken Boundaries

Broken Rebel Brotherhood: Complete Series Box set

Broken Rebel Brotherhood: Next Generation

Broken Hearts

Broken Wings

Broken Mind

Bastards and Badges

Stark Revenge

Slade's Fall

Jett's Guard

Soulless Kings MC

Fender

Joker

Piston

Greaser

Riker

Trainwreck

Squirrel

Gibson

Satan's Legacy MC

Snow's Angel

Toga's Demons

Magic's Torment

ALSO BY NICOLE CYPHER

For a comprehensive list, check out Nicole's website

The Darker Places Series:

DESIRED

DEPLORABLE

DETHRONED

DEMOLISHED

JULIUS

Soulless Kings MC:

FENDER

JOKER

Gruco Crime Family Series:

HIS PROMISE

HIS PET

HIS PRIZE

HIS PUPPET

HIS PROPERTY

Standalone Novels:

UNHINGED

VICIOUS KNIGHT

PROLOGUE

They say your life flashes before your eyes at the moment just before death. They fucking lied.

Fender

Slick. Wet. Hot. Perfect.

That's the only way to describe the pussy I'm buried in. Charlie moans and the sound seems to echo around us in flawless rhythm with the headboard banging against the wall.

"That's it, baby," I growl as I reach between our bodies and rub circles over her clit with my thumb.

Charlie's eyes resemble an emerald in its purest form, and I'm lost, drowning in a sea of green. They widen and her pupils dilate the second her orgasm begins. Tingles race down my spine, and my body tenses as I join her.

We explode together, and the sounds we've created die down. My heart is pounding, and her breathing is labored. I roll off of her, carrying her with me and tucking her into my side.

"Holy shit, Fender."

"What?" I ask, a grin tugging at my lips. She always says the same thing after we fuck. Always.

"It gets better every—"

"Fender, get the fuck out here!"

The pounding on my door and the urgency in Piston's voice has me springing from the bed and grabbing my gun from the nightstand. That's when it registers. Gunshots, yelling, glass shattering.

"Fender! Now!" Piston's fist is an inch away from my face when I throw open the door. "Black Savages stormed the club. Get dressed and c'mon!"

I glance over my shoulder and see Charlie shoving her legs into her jeans. Her ass is encased in the black lace I pulled off her body with my teeth not a half hour ago. I hate to see her cover her flesh, but I can't think about that right now.

"Get in the fuckin' closet and don't come out. Not for anything." I grip her bicep and drag her to the door in the corner of the room, throw it open and shove her in.

"Maybe I can talk to them. Maybe I—"

"No. They're past talking and so am I." I crush her lips in a bruising kiss before shutting the door in her face.

I dress as quickly as I can and mentally prepare for what I'm about to see. Certainly nothing good. I make my way down the hall, my gun cocked and ready to blow away any Savage that gets in my path.

I just pray it's not Dyno. It would be great to take out the president of the Black Savages, but I can't do that to Charlie. I can't kill her dad.

I round the corner into the main room of the clubhouse and am shocked at the carnage. The floor is littered with broken liquor bottles and booze. There's also blood and bodies, and it's hard to tell what club the deceased belong to.

"Fender!"

I whirl toward the voice and see my father, his shirt soaked in blood, kneeling on the floor. My mother is cocooned in his arms, her body limp. Everything else melts away. The shouting, the gunfire, the mayhem. Cold calm washes over me as I walk toward my parents, ignoring the bullets whizzing past my head. Maybe I'd get lucky and one would take me out so I wouldn't have to face what I know is coming.

Time speeds up the closer I get. I drop to my knees. "Where are you hit?"

My father's stare is blank, empty. When he doesn't respond, I run my hands over his chest to determine if the blood is his or all from the hole I can now see in my mother's head. I don't allow myself to feel the loss. I can't afford to fall apart right now. My fingers hit a soft spot, a hole, on the left side of my father's chest. I rip the sleeves from his shirt and stuff the fabric in the hole to slow the bleeding. He hisses in pain, but that's his only reaction.

"Stay here," I shout at him, praying he hears what I'm saying. "I'll be back."

I lunge to my feet and storm into the middle of the room. I take a deep breath and find my first target. I point the gun and squeeze the trigger, not stopping until I've systematically taken out every Black Savage still standing, emptying the clip in the process.

"What the fuck was that?" Piston asks, walking through the bodies, kicking a few as he goes.

"Who'd we lose?" I survey the scene, trying to answer my own question.

"Stunner, Carbon, Phantom," Piston rubs his head, leaving a streak of blood. He's looking around, same as me. His head stops moving, and his gaze lands on something behind me. "Aw, fuck."

I slowly turn around, needing to see what he sees, and

instantly regret it. My father is slumped over, both my parents dead. It's fitting, I suppose. They lived for the club and died for it. It's what they would've wanted, to go out together in a blaze of glory.

Bang!

I pivot around at the gunshot, shocked to hear it because I thought the chaos was over. Charlie's standing there, her eyes wide, her arms straight, the gun in her hand. I follow her gaze to the man she just killed. Sharp, the Black Savages' Sergeant at Arms, is lying on the floor with a bullet hole between his eyes.

"He was gonna kill you," she mumbles.

"You need to leave," Piston demands. "You don't belong here."

My eyes dart back and forth between the woman I love and my best friend. He's absolutely right. She shouldn't be here. Especially now. But I don't have it in me to make her leave.

"Did you do this?" Joker shouts from behind Piston, directing the question at Charlie. "Precious Black Savages' princess coordinates Soulless Kings' massacre. Isn't spreading your legs enough to secure your place?"

Charlie's arms drop to her sides, and the gun clanks to the floor. She's staring at me, silently begging me to defend her, protect her from the lies my brother's spewing. Problem is, I can't. What if he's right?

"Get the fuck out!" Joker shouts, pointing toward the exit.

Charlie's eyes well with tears as she turns and runs out the front door. In my twenty-three years on this Earth, I've stared down the barrel of a gun more times than I can count, and it doesn't hold a candle to what I'm experiencing right now.

I was born to be a Soulless King, raised to be a ruthless, loyal motherfucker. None of that prepared me for this moment. Nothing could make losing so much any easier to swallow.

They say your life flashes before your eyes at the moment just before death. They fucking lied.

Your life flashes before your eyes at the moment you lose everything you live for.

CHAPTER ONE

They told me I couldn't outrun my demons. At least I tried.

Charlie

Four years later...

My black dress itches. There's a tag in the collar that scratches my skin with every movement, but I welcome the irritation and give it all my attention. Anything to distract myself from the steps I take toward the church and the heavy door I'm not sure I'll be able to open with my shaky hands.

I stand outside it, staring at the metal ring attached to it as a knocker and wonder if anyone ever uses it.

"Excuse me," a couple says from behind me, and I jump. I spin to face them and take a step to my right to get out of their way. Neither of them seem familiar, and the dull ache that's been in my stomach ever since I got the news twists into a heavy blow. Would I have known them if I had stayed? Would they know me?

The man opens the door and ushers the woman in, glancing at me as if to see if I've worked up the courage to walk in or not. There's a distastefulness to his expression, with his turned down lips and slightly wrinkled nose, that makes me think he *does* know me.

I duck my head and hurry inside, trying not to read the thoughts of everyone who comes into contact with me today, but I fail. I can see it on their faces after they squint and decipher who I am.

Traitor.

Deserter.

Dishonorable.

I scurry into the room filled with pews and a casket at the head of them. It's open, and it's weird to think of that as a possibility. I always saw my father going out with gunfire, his enemies shooting him repeatedly in the head to ensure the Black Savages' king was dead. Or maybe someone blowing up our—*my family's*—house or slitting his throat as he sleeps. I didn't picture something as human as a stroke killing my father… my daddy.

Tears well in my eyes, and I stand off to the side for a moment to regain my composure. He wouldn't have wanted me to cry. It's a sign of surrender, and that is not something we do in my family.

I wipe underneath my eyes and breathe in through my nose to steady myself. I straighten my spine and square my shoulders before going back to the center isle and walking up to the front row where I belong, ignoring all of the whispers and stares that fill the room like locusts as I pass by.

My mother is already there, along with my cousin Maggie, sister Sylvia, and Aunt Annabelle. I pause in front of my mother, but she doesn't look at me. Her eyes are hardened as she stares right through me to get her point across.

I am not welcome here.

"Charlotte," Maggie whispers, patting the seat beside her. I sigh and walk to Maggie before sitting on the pew next to her.

"I'm so glad you're here." She forces a smile and takes my hand, but I don't have the heart to return the gesture. I never have. My father always told me my biggest downfall was my inability to fake my emotions. I'm not a charmer. What you see is what you get.

Maggie makes me wish I was different, though. She's the closest tie I have to this life and the only one who doesn't seem to hate me for leaving it. She's the one who called to tell me my father died. I'm not sure I would've known otherwise.

Leaving the family didn't just mean leaving my mother and father. It meant leaving the Black Savages. Loyalty is at the epicenter of their core beliefs, and leaving is like turning your back on them. It's betrayal, treason. Forbidden.

My father must have hated me before he died, but I can't help but notice he never sent anyone after me. That's always made me fear he knew the reason I left or what I'd done, but I can't let my mind go there. Not today.

Today, I am not my father's embarrassment. Today, I am my daddy's little girl.

The Black Savages' chaplain does the service, and he goes on about all of the good qualities my father possessed that the club's principles are founded on. He talks about an afterlife and pretends my father was a good man who's being rewarded with streets of gold. Or maybe he isn't pretending. Maybe he believes it. I wish I could.

He hands the podium over to members of the MC, and Dad's top three guys take turns telling stories about their prez and giving their respects. I laugh along with the congregation of bikers and associates when Missile tells a story about my dad when he first joined the MC. The pain in my stomach lessens hearing it.

I was scared I'd forget the happy memories of Daddy, but hearing about this side of him opens up a part of my mind that floods me with warmth. He taught me how to ride my first bike. Not a bicycle like most little girls, no. A small little

Kawasaki where I immediately revved the engine too much and threw the bike out from under me. Daddy laughed, and after the initial shock, I laughed with him.

Leal, my father's right-hand man and the apparent new president of the club, comes up last. Tears escape his eyes as he talks about my father like he was the most honorable man on the face of this earth. Leal has been my dad's best friend since before I was born, and my father respected him so much he gave him his road name, which is an English word for loyalty. That's the strongest trait anyone can possess, and Leal carried it like a badge of honor. He pins his eyes on me as he talks about Dad during the birth of his first child, me, and how it changed his life forever.

He talks like he's speaking directly to me, and I force myself not to take my eyes away. My cheeks heat, but my face remains impassive. As much as I hate the eyes on me, I'm glad he's doing this. He speaks with compassion and it sounds as if he's welcoming me back without saying the words.

He moves on to another subject, and I sit perfectly still, only giving him a single nod as he finishes and leaves the podium. He nods back, and I wish I could run up and throw my arms around him. I would cry into his chest and tell him how much I miss Dad. I'd tell him how I never wanted to abandon them, but I had no choice. I couldn't take this life anymore. I didn't want it.

My blood relatives are up next, and I watch their mouths move but don't hear a word they say. My hands are sweaty, and the tips of my fingers throb with my heartbeat. I don't know if they've ever done that before.

The chaplain asks if anyone else would like to say a few words, and I take a deep breath before standing. My mother gives me a pointed stare as if to say *sit down,* but I ignore it and walk behind the podium.

I practiced this speech on the drive from my new home in

South Carolina to my old one in Oregon. I've rehearsed it more times than I can remember, but now that I'm up here, my mind goes blank. Cotton fills my mouth and soaks up all the moisture.

I clear my throat into the microphone.

"Hello and thank you for coming," I say, as if I'm the one welcoming them here. *I'm* not even welcome here. "As some of you may know, I'm Dyno's eldest daughter. We didn't always see eye to eye, but..."

Fuck. I'm crying. The first tear has spilled over, and my throat feels full of imaginary gunk that I know is only emotion.

Never cry, baby girl. Crying is weak. Crying is surrender. Black Savages don't do that.

"But I loved him very much." My voice cracks, and I wipe my cheeks on my itchy dress's sleeve.

I scan the faces of the crowd, seeing mostly disgust but also a little bit of pity. My eyes land on a man at the back, his suit standing out but probably hiding his identity from most of the crowd. He doesn't even look like Fender in it, but maybe that's because it's been four years. He looks so much older now, like it's been twenty. The mischievous smile I used to admire isn't there, but one look at his hardened face and I can tell he hasn't sported it in a long time. Probably not since that day. His dark hair is combed back, and his beard is neatly trimmed. His gray eyes lock with mine, but no emotion comes over his face.

Why is he here? It's the first question that comes to my mind, but the second overshadows it.

Does he hate me too?

"Thank you," I say into the microphone, abandoning the idea of rectifying my failed speech. I hear people murmur, but I keep my head down as I walk back to my seat. I sit next to Maggie again, and she squeezes my hand and says nothing as I cry. There isn't any hope of holding the tears back now.

They flow down my face with ease, and this time, I don't wipe them away.

It's a bitter kind of irony that this is exactly what I know my father wanted, for me to come home. To join my family again and be the daughter he always wanted me to be. To pledge my loyalty to the Black Savages and never stray from that again. I don't think he ever knew just how much I betrayed him, but I don't know how much it matters anymore. I cry harder and cover my mouth to keep sobs from escaping.

I surrender, Daddy.

When the chaplain wraps up the service, I've calmed down enough that my vision isn't completely blurry. I turn my head around to peer at the back of the room, looking for Fender, but he's gone. I let out a sigh of relief. I doubt he was here to pay his respects. He probably just wanted to make sure my father was really dead, but whatever the reason, I'm glad he's gone now.

The last thing my father said to me before I packed a bag and left was that you can't outrun your demons.

At least I tried.

CHAPTER TWO

I need answers. But first, I need the courage to ask the questions.

Fender

"What the fuck are you wearing?"

I flip Margo the bird as I stalk past the bar.

"If I were a decade younger," she cackles, which only sets off a coughing fit from years of smoking Marlboro Reds.

Margo is Burly's ol' Lady and a mother hen to boot, if mother hens wore denim and leather. She took it upon herself to 'look out for me' after my mom died, and if I'm being honest, I don't hate it.

I unlock my room at the clubhouse and toss my tie on the floor as I enter. I strip out of the suit in record time and decide to take a quick shower to wash the fancy off of me before I head back out to party with my brothers. As the water sluices over my head, I conjure up an image of Charlie in her black dress and the look on her face as she tried to talk about her father.

My cock hardens, and as much as I need the release, I'm not giving it to myself. After the last few hours, I need a warm pussy to do the work for me. When I step out of the shower, I grab my discarded jeans from earlier and pull them on my still damp legs and finish dressing with what I assume, based on the smell, is a clean tee and my cut.

When I enter the bar area of the clubhouse, I scan the room for Piston and find him lounging on a couch with his head thrown back and a blonde between his hairy thighs. Shaking my head, I step up to the worn wooden counter and watch as Margo hands a skinny prospect an uncapped bottle of Hop Venom.

"Prospect," I growl when he starts to walk away.

"Yo," he says when he turns around with the bottle to his lips.

I hear Margo mumble 'oh shit' behind me, and I can't help the grin that tugs at the corner of my lips. This jack-off is going to give me exactly what I need to calm the beast clamoring to get out.

"Yo?" I snarl as I advance on him. "You talk to your mama with that mouth?"

"Uh, y-ye—"

With lightning quick speed, I grab him by his shirt and throw him against the bar as if he weighs nothing. Wrapping a hand around the back of his head, I shove his face in the wood and am disappointed by the whine that escapes his mouth.

"You wanna wear our patch, you show some motherfucking respect. Margo isn't your bitch, and I'm not the punk from down the street." I lean in close so I can get a good look at the fear in his eyes. "I'm the goddamn president of the Soulless Kings, and if I catch you pulling that shit again, not only will your prospecting days be over, but you'll wish you were never born."

The prospect swallows, and if it weren't for the Guns N' Roses belting from the sound system, I probably would have heard the kerthunk of his throat. I've seen this kid before, but never at a party. His black leather vest is a wannabe's cut, void of any patches. Piston usually oversees prospects, but if this is the shit he's bringing in maybe I need to be more involved.

"What's your name?"

"T-T-Tyler," he stammers.

"Tyler, you better grow some balls real quick if you want to survive this life." I yank him upright. "Now, take a look around." He doesn't listen so I smack him upside the head. "When your president gives you an order, you fucking obey." Tyler quickly turns to scan the room. "See all those pretty half-naked chicks?" He bobs his head. "You wanna girl to be your bitch, you get one of them."

"Y-Yes, sir." Tyler turns back toward me, and I'm glad to see some of the color is returning to his cheeks.

"Much better. So Tyler, Piston give you a handle yet?"

"A handle, sir?"

I roll my eyes at his complete lack of understanding. "Yeah, a fucking handle. A road name." When his stare remains blank, I clarify the only way I know how. "A fucking nickname."

"Oh, uh, no, sir." Tyler chuckles to cover his nervousness.

"Ya got one now. From here on out, you're Trainwreck, cause lord fucking knows that's exactly what you'll be."

His eyes narrow for a split second before he masks his anger. "Trainwreck." He repeats the name a few times as if seeing how it feels rolling off his tongue. "All due respect, *sir*, I ain't no trainwreck and I'll prove it to you."

His attitude pisses me off and at the same time gives me a glimmer of hope that Piston's not completely running our club into wimp territory.

"It's Fender, or better yet, prez. Call me 'sir' one more time, and your nuts are gonna get up close and personal with your throat. Got me?" He nods. "Get the fuck outta my sight."

He turns away from me, and I let him think he's getting away before I call out to him.

"And Trainwreck?" His body stiffens and he glances over his shoulder. "You're working the bar with Margo tomorrow night."

Trainwreck's shoulders sag, but he nods and returns to his task of escaping me.

"Poor kid doesn't stand a chance."

I slide onto a bar stool and face Margo. The corners of her eyes are crinkled which tells me she's trying not to laugh at what just happened. I shake my head at her.

"Maybe, maybe not." I grab the bottle of Armored Fist she slides at me and take a swig before slamming it on the wood in front of me. "Either way, it's sure gonna be fun to watch."

"Fender, if your fath—"

"Not now, Margo," I bark. "Today has been shit, and the only thing I want is to get drunk and fuck. I don't need any of your sage advice muddying the waters."

"Too damn bad," she snaps. She's the only one in this place who can get away with that shit. "I'm gonna say what I have to say, and you're gonna fuckin' listen."

"You've got two minutes and then I'm walking away."

"I only need one." She wipes the bar down with her rag, as she often does when she's going to get all *feelings* on me. "Your parents were great people. Loyal, strong, the best mama and daddy a kid could ask for, but they failed you, too." I'd been staring into my beer, but with that statement, my head snaps up. "Hear me out." She holds her hand up to stop the protest on my lips. "There's a great big world out there, and you're not limited to this little corner. Don't get me wrong, the Soulless Kings are my family, my home and I would do anything for them, but I didn't start out here. If Burly hadn't spread his wings, so to speak, I wouldn't be here. Now I get that that girl is supposed to be poison, the enemy, but Fender, I saw how you were with her all those years ago. And then everything turned to shit. Your parents were gunned down, she left. After that night, you changed. You hardened."

"It's never just a minute," I mumble.

"Shut it. I know you went to Dyno's funeral, and I'm guessing by the granite hard look on your face when you walked back in here that she was there. You've spent so much time listening to Joker and Piston and the other brothers tell you that she's no good, that she set you up, but what do you believe?"

I have no answer to her question, no response to her words. They swirl around in my mind until my head feels like it's going to explode from a deadly combination of fury, confusion and pain. I lift my beer and down the remaining contents. The bitter brew doesn't even begin to quiet my demons.

"Gimme another. And two shots of tequila."

I slide my empty bottle toward Margo, and she tosses it in the trash where it clanks against the rest of the empties. Another bottle appears in front of me along with the double shot glasses, filled to the brim. I down the shots in rapid succession and savor the burn before grabbing the beer and turning away from her. Time to find the other half of the cure to what ails me.

I scan the room for a few minutes, not finding anyone that looks appealing, when it hits me that it's an impossible task. Who I want and who is available are two very different things. I settle on the next best thing when I spot Tina, with her short black hair and her denim-clad ass. She's not Charlie, but she'll do in a pinch.

I sidle up to her and wrap my arms around her waist, pressing my cock into her back as she sways her hips to the music. I close my eyes and let the friction between us do its job. Tina turns around, and her tits strain against the lace tank she's wearing. Her nipples are hard and visible. I bend to capture one between my teeth and pinch the other.

Tina's head is thrown back, and she's grinding her pelvis into my thigh, seeking the release I'm not ready to give. I try to yank her back by her hair, but it's too short to get a good grip. Growling, I stoop to swing her into my arms and carry her to my room.

"Damn, Fender, a girl could get used to this," she purrs into my ear as she's sucking on the lobe.

"Don't."

I kick the door shut behind us and stroll to the bed where I toss her down. She laughs and the sound is like fingernails on a chalkboard. She's not the woman I want, and that's not the laugh I want to hear.

"Why not, baby? You know you like what I do to you."

Tina scrambles to her knees and reaches out to me, dragging me forward and mashing her lips against mine. Tina's cunt is the only one that hasn't been plugged up by any of my brothers, which is the only reason she's ever been allowed in my room, in my bed.

"I'm not your fucking baby." I grip her wrists and hold them above her head.

"Whatever you say, Fender." Tina squirms and I let her go.

"Take your fucking clothes off," I demand.

Tina strips and I can't help but notice the track marks on her arms. I'm guessing she's high right now, but I'm too much of a prick to give a damn about her inability to make smart decisions. Because fucking me is not a smart decision. Not when I'm wishing she were someone else.

I unbutton my jeans and shove them down until they pool at my feet. My cock springs free, and Tina's eyes immediately seek it out. She licks her lips and practically bounces with excitement.

"Suck my cock."

I take a step back and point to the floor in front of me.

Tina does as she's told and kneels on the carpet. When she leans forward and her pink tongue darts out of her mouth, I brace myself for the contact. Tina swirls saliva around the head of my cock, and when she makes no move to take me in, I thrust my hips forward until I ram the back of her throat.

"I said, suck. My. Cock."

Tina finally starts to move her head, and with each pass over my length, she lets her teeth scrape the sensitive flesh. Some men might not enjoy the pain, but I'm not some men. The pain is the punishment I deserve for letting my dick anywhere near someone who's not *her*.

Tina moans and the vibrations make my dick twitch. Too close to blowing my load and knowing she deserves something in return, I lift her up and shove her on the bed.

"On your stomach."

Tina rolls over and her ass is sticking up, begging to be smacked. The crack of my palm leaves a red mark and Tina whimpers. I spank her four more times before I spear her pussy with two fingers, not bothering to see if she's ready. Tina's moans fill the room and make it difficult for me to picture her as anyone else.

"Shut up." I smack her ass again.

When her walls clench around my fingers, I replace them with my cock and pound into her from behind. Tina's knuckles are white as she grasps at the blanket underneath her. Mine are white as my fingertips dig into the flesh at her hips. My orgasm is close, but something is missing. Something is holding me back.

"Fen-Fender... gonna come."

Tina's wails reverberate off the walls, and her pussy clenches with her release. When she collapses onto the bed and I'm still hard as a rock, I flip her onto her back and crawl up her body to fuck her face. I need to fucking come and this ain't done until I do.

Tina lets me bang her mouth while she plays with my

balls. My eyes slide closed, and I imagine another set of lips sucking me, another pair of hands pushing me to my limit. With that picture in my head, the tell-tale tingle races down my spine and I fill Tina's mouth with my cum.

When I'm spent, I fall to the bed at her side and stare at the ceiling. It's always crazy how pussy can make you feel so good and so fucking terrible at the same time.

"Get out," I growl and push Tina away from me.

"C'mon, Fender, let me stay," Tina whines.

"Get. Out."

"You're a fucking asshole," she spits out.

After she grabs her clothes, she storms out of the room without getting dressed. I stay right where I'm at, thinking, staring, regretting. As I lie there, one thing becomes crystal clear: I can't keep doing this.

I need answers. But first, I need the courage to ask the questions.

CHAPTER THREE

He was mine, and I was his, and now I'm no one's.

Charlie

My mother, my sister, and I all sit around the kitchen table, eggs and bacon in front of each of us. No one has said a word. Sylvia has only taken two bites, my mother holds her coffee cup in front of her face and takes a sip on occasion, looking off into space, and I move scrambled eggs around with my fork. I don't know how any of us could possibly be hungry right now.

After what feels like too long, Sylvia's fork clanks on the plate and she asks, "Are we really not going to address the elephant in the room?"

I let out a sigh of relief and set my fork down before lacing my fingers and resting them on the table. Finally, we can get this over with.

"This is a time to mourn your father, Sylvia. Not… other things."

"Can't she go stay in a hotel or something?" She turns to me. "Or better yet, go back to wherever the hell you came from."

"This *is* where I come from."

Sylvia huffs and rolls her eyes.

"What? Am I somehow less of Dad's daughter because I wanted to be on my own for a few years? Do I not deserve to mourn? If you want me to fuck off, so be it." I stand and throw a pointed look at my mother. "At least you have the courage to tell me."

I turn to walk away, but Mom's coffee mug slams on the table. I glance at the spilled liquid before moving my gaze to her hardened eyes. "Sit. Down."

I glower a few moments before I plop into the seat, my fists clenched at my sides. She's the one who asked me to come stay at the house for the time being. "It's what your father would have wanted," she'd said, although her face was hard as stone. It gave me hope that maybe she wanted to forgive me, but obviously she just wanted to make me uncomfortable. I would've been perfectly fine staying in a hotel and trying to make my amends from a distance. Now I'm stuck on Black Savages' property surrounded by people who hate me.

The door off the side of the kitchen creaks open, and I swivel to find Leal coming inside. He wipes his boots on the mat and grins at us like he can't feel the thick tension in the room. "Mornin' ladies."

"Hey Uncle Leal." Sylvia springs to her feet and bubbles with affection as she goes over and hugs him. It seems she's forgotten the tension too. "What are you doing here?"

He hugs her back and, when he lets go, he strides over to the countertop. "I was hoping to snag me a bite of your mama's cookin'." He plucks a piece of bacon and lifts it as if to say cheers. "And I'm in luck."

He's not really here for that, and we all know it. They're several club whores who stay in the clubhouse that would cook for him if he wanted. He's checking on us, and the sentiment is sweet. I've always liked Leal.

"Hey, Char, how you doin'?"

I shrug. "I'm okay."

My lack of manipulating my facial expressions betrays me, and I can tell by the creases around his eyes that he knows I'm not okay. He gives me a kind smile anyway. "Are you planning on staying a while or do you need to head back?"

Head back. I wish there was something to head back to. I never even called my job at the shop to tell them I quit or that I planned on leaving the state, so that bridge is burned. My apartment is a one bedroom with shit furniture and a Harley Davidson lamp I could probably live without.

No, I don't have anything to go back to. But I'm not sure there's anything for me here anymore, either. "I'm not sure what I'm doing actually." I give a tight smile and he nods, this time frowning.

"Well, let's get together soon, okay? Catch up."

"Of course."

He stays a little while, making small talk with my mom and sister while I stare off into space trying to decide what the next stage of my life will be. I never planned to come back here. I never planned to come back to *him*.

He hates me.

They hate me.

Sometimes even *I* hate me.

I'm not even sure who I betrayed worse anymore. Fender, for simply being my father's daughter and belonging to the people who raided his club, or the Black Savages for killing one of our own and taking off.

But they don't know about what I did… right?

"I'm gonna take off," I say, my face hot as I stand.

Leal turns to me. "You need a ride?"

"Nah, I'm gonna take my bike."

My bike. Fuck, I have missed her. Four years without the

wind whipping through my hair while my legs straddle a five-hundred-pound beast is way too long.

His eyebrows raise. "All right but be sure to get one of the guys to give it a tune up… if it still runs."

I nod and head out the door without another word to my sister or mom. When I get to the garage, I pull the door up and comfort washes through me at the grating sound it makes and the weight under my arms. It's weird the things you miss without ever realizing it.

I pluck my keys off the hook and try not to look at my dad's bike as I find mine exactly where I left it. I wonder what'll happen to his. Will Sylvia get it? My mom? One of the brothers? Or will it just sit in the garage and collect dust like mine has?

I wipe some of the dust off the seat, but don't fuck with it too long. I'd rather not stay here another second. Fitting the key into the ignition, I bite my lip and praise God when my baby starts up.

My chest squeezes as I pull out of the garage and head to town. There's no way I'm asking a brother to give my bike a tune up, not right now when everyone hates me. I could do it myself, but that would require me to spend more time on Black Savages property than I want to right now.

So instead I ride the ten miles into town, forcing myself not to show my teeth as I smile so a bug can't stain them. It feels so good to be on my bike, I almost don't stop going. I could just ride off into the proverbial sunset, never stopping until I reached a place that felt like home. But that would defeat the purpose of coming back here, and the hard truth is I have no home away from here. This life is where I belong, whether they want me or not. And I should know because I've been searching for a new home for years and have come up empty.

I search out a garage I haven't been to before so, hopefully, I won't run into anyone who knew me before I left. I find one with a newer looking building on the edge of town. Infinite Motors. What a corny ass name.

I pull the bike into the lot and park before hopping off and heading to the main entrance. A bell dings as I push the door open.

No one is at the counter, so I walk up to it and lean against the granite, tapping my foot as I wait.

The door behind the counter swings open and out comes a man with gray eyes that haunt my dreams... and sometimes my nightmares.

"Fender," I say, standing up straight. My foot stops tapping, and I glance down at my rugged clothes, covered in dust. My cheeks heat before I can realize how ridiculous I am for it. He isn't someone I should try to impress.

He stalks to the counter, and his face hardens to an impossible degree. I don't remember him looking so serious. He was so much more... boy, when I knew him. Worlds away from the man standing before me.

"What do you want?" Inside, I flinch from his sharp tone. Outside, my face is impassive.

"Since when are you working at a garage? The club's shop not good enough for you? Or is money just that tight?" My words are just as sharp, but I ask the questions more out of curiosity than insult. I don't even want to insult him, but I can't help it with the way he's talking to me. It's a defense mechanism I've never been able to shake. I wonder if he remembers that.

He snarls. "I own the place. Tell me what you want or get the fuck out."

My eyes widen in surprise. He owns a garage now? I guess I shouldn't be so surprised. He's a damn good mechanic, and it's always been his passion. The cut he's wearing is a clear marker for Soulless Kings, so I have to wonder if the garage is his or *theirs*. Not that it matters.

"Never mind, I'll go somewhere else."

I turn and prepare to leave, but Fender is around the counter and blocking me before I make it more than two feet to the door. He pushes me back, and I stumble to the counter, his hands slamming down on either side of me to block me in. His face is inches from mine, and I know it's out of intimidation and not lust, but my core starts to heat anyway. I can smell him. Oil and exhaust coupled with a scent only belonging to him.

Another one of the things I didn't realize I missed.

"Are you really gonna pretend you didn't know this was my garage?"

I narrow my eyes. "I *didn't* know that this was your garage, Fender. I wouldn't have come here if I did."

"Don't call me that."

"What should I call you then? Chri—"

Before I can get the word out, his hand circles my throat and he squeezes. Not enough so that I *can't* breathe, but enough that it's uncomfortable.

"Don't call me *anything*."

I wrap my hands around his wrist and tug, but when he squeezes tight I force my hands to my sides and close my eyes. I feel his breath skate over my cheek, and I shudder. "I don't know why you came back, but consider this my one and only warning. Stay the fuck away from me and my club. This isn't Black Savages territory anymore, Charlie. You're on the wrong side of the tracks."

He releases my throat and I take a few deep breaths, being sure I don't gasp and show he's affected me. Then I open my eyes and stare into his which are still so close to me. A patch on his cut rubs against my nipple and hardens it, although I'm certain he isn't doing it intentionally.

"You know exactly why I'm here," I say, a little too breathlessly. "I saw you at the funeral."

"Funeral? This whole time I was thinking it was a celebration."

This time the wince is external, and I turn my face away. There was a time when I loved this man. I let him hold me, and I let him see me cry. He was mine, and I was his, and now I'm no one's. It fucking hurts. He didn't come to the funeral for me. He came to smite my father.

"Fuck you, Fender." There isn't enough animosity in my tone for my liking, but I hold on to my dignity. He'll never see me cry again.

He leans into my neck and goosebumps spread over my flesh. "I've already been there… And look what it cost me."

He sounds pained, and this time I picture him with the wince. The way his breath caresses my flesh, I'm almost convinced he's about to kiss me there, but he pulls back abruptly and walks around the counter. He turns his head to peer back at me with his hand on the door. "This is the one and only pass I'm giving you. Don't come on our turf again."

He's through the door and I'm standing there alone a moment later. I'm frozen for what must be minutes but feels like years.

I shouldn't be surprised.

I knew he hated me.

I saw the look in his eyes the day I left.

And still, my heart feels like it's breaking into a thousand pieces all over again. I take deep breaths in through my nose and close my eyes long enough that by the time I'm walking back to my bike, I'm walking tall. I'm not the broken girl he made me four years ago, and he isn't the boy who stole my heart.

I guess it's goodbye for real this time.

CHAPTER FOUR

If my parents being murdered was the knife thrust in my gut, Charlie leaving was it being twisted, shredding my insides until they were unrecognizable.

Fender

"What the fuck was that all about?"

I glare at Joker, who's supposed to be working on the vintage 1946 Indian Chief. I'd called him in because the customer wanted the bike restored, and while I'm a great fucking mechanic, restoration isn't my thing. Joker on the other hand can bring anything back to life.

"Fuckin' hell, brother. I can see it all over your face. You wanna hit that again. Are you forgetting the shitstorm she brought to our door?"

My control snaps. I storm across the garage and get within inches of Joker's face. He shows no fear of my rage, which doesn't surprise me but does increase my fury.

"Don't for one second think I've forgotten that night," I snarl. "How could I? My parents are fucking dead. Not only that but everyone has made it crystal fucking clear what they think of that bitch and I've listened." I narrow my eyes and back up a step. "But I'm still your prez and you will not fucking question me again. Ya got me?"

"Uh, should I come back?"

I whirl around and see Piston standing in the doorway I walked through just moments ago. He's got a hardened look on his face, but his glare is directed at Joker, not me. That's why he's my VP. He's been in complete agreement with the others regarding Charlie's role in that night, but at the end of the day, he's loyal to me.

"Nah, you're just in time. Fender here is explaining how he doesn't want to dip his dick in the prodigal daughter of the Black Savages."

I glance back at Joker and take in the sneer on his face. Joker's a knife wielding son of a bitch and a hell of a Sergeant at Arms, but his road name fits him like a glove. Sometimes, he never knows when to fucking let things go. Usually, it's something stupid and gives the brothers a good laugh, but this shit about Charlie is getting old.

"Ah, I thought that's who I saw sitting outside when I pulled up." Piston scratches the side of his nose, a gesture I know means he's about to say something I won't fucking like. "All due respect, but why is she still upright?"

"Goddammit!" I roar as I lift my leg and kick the bike at Joker's station, knocking it to the ground with a rattling thud.

"That's just great." Piston chuckles and saunters toward me. "Get pissed and break shit. That's really gonna solve the problem."

"Shut it. You know we can fix it," I scoff.

I saunter to my station, my rage simmering just beneath my skin. As much as breaking shit let's me release some of it, Piston's right. Infinite Motors is one of several businesses owned by the Soulless Kings, but it's my baby and I should treat it as such. I spin around to face them again.

"Just go home, both of you." I return my attention to the

bike I was working on when the bell chimed letting me know we had a customer.

"Jesus Christ, you call me down here and now you're sending me away," Joker mumbles as he puts his shit away, slamming his toolbox drawers.

"Joker, enough," Piston snaps, clearly aware of my tenuous grip on sanity.

I keep my back to both of them, taking deep breaths as I listen to them leave. When the bell chimes signaling their exit, I whirl around and throw the wrench in my hand at the wall, where it bounces off with a thud, leaving a hole in its wake.

I need to be alone so I lock up the shop. I've had to be strong, ruthless, since the night my parents died and Charlie walked out, but it hasn't been without a cost. Mostly to myself and my fucked up head.

The sound of the lock clicking into place transports me back to that night. I've locked so much of my memories away in a steel vault in my skull. I've had to, but in an instant, they all come flooding back, assaulting me with precise blows designed to bring me to my knees.

I flip the switch next to the swinging door behind the counter as I pass through, bathing the shop in darkness. Many people are afraid of the dark. Not me. I relish it, the ability it provides me to forget everything else around me and just be, the cover it provides when the Soulless Kings have to strike, the anonymity we get when others can't make us out because of the inky blackness.

Right now, though, all the darkness is giving me is the opportunity to dwell on things I can't change. Fucking Charlie, gunshots ringing out, my mother covered in blood, my father trying to protect her, death, carnage, betrayal, loyalty. The night the world stopped is burned into my brain, and no matter how many deeds I do as president, I can't scrub them away or replace them.

If my parents being murdered was the knife thrust in my gut, Charlie leaving was it being twisted, shredding my insides until they were unrecognizable. Joker and Piston's voices have echoed in my head, yelling that Charlie had betrayed me, had set me up, set the club up and orchestrated the slaughter that took place.

At the time, I didn't believe them, not really, but then she fled the state and there's no denying that was suspicious. Couple that with the constant reminder from my brothers that she's responsible, and I started to question everything I'd ever known.

Don't get me wrong, there was never a part of me that thought a relationship with Charlie was going to be easy, at least not when it came to the rivalry between the Soulless Kings and Black Savages, but growing up in an MC isn't easy. I'd been young and dumb and had hoped that we loved each other enough to make it work, to overcome any obstacle our world threw at us. I was wrong. So fucking wrong.

After burying my parents, without my girl, I poured my soul into proving myself worthy of becoming the president of the Soulless Kings. I stole, fought, fucked, killed. I did it all. No task was too dirty for my hands, and after six months, I'd earned the title.

As president, I vowed to do whatever it took to get revenge on the Black Savages, to hold them accountable for the bloodshed. I told myself that if Charlie was found to be responsible, I could punish her, I could do whatever was necessary to make her pay. But she'd been gone. Maybe it's a good thing she left because despite reassurances to my brothers and myself, I'm not sure I could avenge my club at her expense. It had never been a problem.

Until now.

She's back and I can no longer ignore the questions that have plagued me for four years. Distance has been the perfect excuse, but it's not a factor anymore. When news of her father's death—pitiful way to go out for an MC President if you ask me—reached me, I'd been battered with so many mixed emotions.

Relief had been swift but had quickly been replaced by dread. A death like Dyno's could bring a club to its knees, and while I hoped that would be the case, I'm not stupid. The Black Savages would bury him and move on, much like we had after the night of the massacre.

I knew his death would be the one thing that could bring Charlie back into my orbit, and I dreaded that like nothing else before in my twenty-seven years. I'd gone to the funeral hoping to get a glimpse of her, praying that I'd see her in a different light, that I'd see the bitch who betrayed me.

I'd gotten part of what I wanted. She is indeed different than the girl I fell in love with, but I don't see a monster when I look at her, no matter how hard I try or how much I want to. The sight of her at the podium, trying to come up with words to honor her father, to honor my enemy, had been a sucker punch to the gut.

I'd wanted to go to her, wrap her in my arms and promise her that life would be okay. I'd also wanted to go to her and fuck her brains out right there in front of God and everyone, so maybe I wasn't thinking straight.

When I'd entered the front of Infinite Motors to greet the customer and saw Charlie standing there, I'm not gonna lie, it took a minute to get my mind right. She may not look exactly like the girl who walked out on me, on us, but there's no denying that she's even better. She's a fucking wide awake wet dream. Hair that reminds me of melted dark chocolate and eyes that reminds me of the luscious greenery up and down the Oregon Coast. That greenery has been witness to so much over time and her eyes mirrored that, so full of heartache, wisdom, unease, fear.

I should have demanded answers right then and there, but I couldn't. Not with Joker in the next room. Instead, I threw up my walls and forced the man I've become to bleed through. I focused on the fact that she'd been trespassing on Soulless Kings' territory. Never mind the fact that she wouldn't have known that as our acquisition of it is relatively recent. Not my problem that she isn't up on current events. But I made it hers.

The corners of my mouth pull into a grin. The look on her face when I gripped her throat was priceless. Charlie has always been a badass. She had to be, growing up the Black Savages' princess, but all of that had fled for a brief moment and she'd been at my mercy. I like her that way. Too much.

I gave her a free pass, the only one she'll ever get, but now I'm second guessing that decision. I had her, literally in my grasp, and I let her go. Am I getting soft? Does she still have her tentacles wrapped around every cell in my body, holding me hostage and pussy whipping me into submission?

No.

My smile falls as the music in the shop shifts. 'Blame It On The Boom Boom' by Black Stone Cherry pumps out of the sound system I installed before opening. Normally, I can handle this song and the memories it brings with it, but not now. Not so soon after seeing Charlie. Not so quickly after memories of that night have overtaken my every thought. Not when it's the song that had been playing as I'd buried myself in her body and my parents had been gunned down.

I lift a screwdriver from my work bench and launch it in the same direction as the wrench. Unlike before, this tool sticks in the wall, and for a second I envision Charlie's shocked expression behind it, blood oozing from the hole it would leave in her skull.

I shake my head to clear my thoughts. Wallowing is a pussy's game. I'm no fucking pussy. I take a deep breath and shove my memories back into the vault I built for them. Shoulders squared, I head out the back door, locking it behind me.

When I straddle my Harley Davidson Road King and rev the engine, the vibration goes straight to my balls. The tingling feeling grounds me in a way nothing else can. I pull out of the parking lot behind our building and point the bike in the direction of my club.

I've waited years to get answers, and if I'm going to do that without other unwanted emotions getting in the way, I'm going to need my brothers. I don't ask much of them. Stay loyal, protect the club, don't get caught. That's always been enough.

Until now.

CHAPTER FIVE

This isn't about us. This isn't even about me. This is about him.

Charlie

"We could... Fender..."

"What did you just say?" I stop abruptly, my boots squeaking on the mall's linoleum floor. Maggie has been talking nonstop since she showed up at my mother's house on her Harley. I managed to tune her out around a half hour ago, but now she has my full attention.

She quirks a brow at me and pops her gum. "I said we could go check out other stores if you wanted or swing by the vendors downtown. What, you too good for the flea markets now or somethin'?"

The tightness in my chest loosens with the breath I let out. Vendor, not Fender. Fuck, I *am* losing my mind.

"No, sorry. That's fine."

Maggie frowns and takes my hand, leading me away so we aren't blocking people. We take the escalator down to the food court, and the smell makes my gut twist and rumble. I haven't eaten today... or yesterday now that I think about it.

She leads me to a table and points at a chair. "Sit."

I narrow my eyes at her tone and don't move. My stubborn side won't let me.

Maggie rolls her eyes. "Damn, girl, you look like you're about to pass out. Will you sit so I know you won't collapse while I go get us some food?"

"I can go." I step around the chair, but pause when my vision goes a little hazy. The smell of all the pizza mixing with orange chicken is making me nauseous.

"Sit. Down." Maggie pulls out a chair for me, and I roll my eyes at her like she's ridiculous before sitting.

I sigh as she leaves and lay my head in my hands with my elbows propped on the table. I'm shit at showing it, but I'm forever grateful for that girl. I don't know how someone could still be friends with me after…

Well, after.

Maggie returns with two giant slices of pizza and sets one down in front of me. My stomach rumbles, and I ignore the sound, hoping she will too. I take my first bite and pretend I don't notice the quizzical look she's giving me.

"What's going on with you?"

I chew the bite as slowly and casually as possible before swallowing. "What do you mean?"

"Are you starving yourself? Is anorexia like the cool thing on the east coast or something?"

I snort and take another bite of pizza. I hold my hand in front of my mouth and answer in between chewing. "No, I just honestly forgot to eat… There's a lot of tension at my mom's."

And plenty of tension coming from *him*.

I swear over the last couple of days, ever since seeing Fender, I've felt like someone's been watching me. Even at home hairs stand on my arms if the curtains in my bedroom are open. But that's ridiculous.

Maggie gives me an apologetic frown. "Sylvia and your mom still aren't coming around?"

I shrug. "Mom says she doesn't want me to leave, but I don't know. To be honest, Mags, I don't feel welcome here. Maybe it'd be better for everyone if I left."

I say it like it's the logical thing to do, and it is. My voice is even and cold, but inside my heart is crushing and I hope she'll tell me not to go. Then at least I'd know one person wanted me to stay.

Maggie glares. "What kind of coward-ass shit is that?"

"Excuse me?"

She shakes her head and picks at her pizza. "You know, when you left the first time, I admired you. I thought you left because you wanted more, and you didn't give a shit about what anyone thought about it. I had no idea it was because you were a *runner*."

I grind my teeth and lean forward. "Take that back."

"No."

"Take it—"

"I'll take it back when you tell me you're not about to walk away with your back hunched. We're your family, Char. So what if some people are pissed? This is where you belong, so make them *un*pissed."

"I wish it were that simple," I mutter, Fender's image flashing through my mind.

"It is."

I consider arguing with her, but if I do that, I'll have to tell her things. Like that my family aren't the people I'm concerned about the most. And that if they knew everything I've done, there would be no chance of them being 'unpissed'.

We eat the rest of our pizza in silence, then continue through the mall. Maggie holds up clothes to me and babbles about who the hell knows what while I humor her by trying on the outfits and even purchasing a few things. I toss glances over my shoulder every few minutes when that same sickening feeling of being watched won't subside. I'm being paranoid.

By the time we leave the mall, several bags in hand, the sun has set. We walk out the wrong door and have to scale around the building for several minutes before we see our bikes parked at the far end of the lot.

All I can think about during our walk are the eyes I feel on me and who I imagine they belong to. That's what this is, isn't it? It isn't paranoia, it's a fantasy.

That's even more wrong.

I give in to the urge I've been fighting all day and clear my throat before peering at Maggie. "Can I ask you something?"

She tosses me a glance and continues toward our bikes, but at a slower pace. "Anything."

"I saw someone the other day who I thought I recognized, and I'm wondering if you remember this guy from when we were younger. His name was like Bumper or Bender or something like that?"

She stops fully and tilts her head at me. "Fender?"

"Yeah, maybe. I'm not sure, to be honest. I think I might have met him at a bar or something years ago."

"Why do you want to know about Fender?"

Her tone is accusatory, and my skin starts to crawl thinking about why that might be. I have no idea what I've missed in the four years since I left, but I know Fender didn't just 'get over' his parents' murders. War between our two clubs has either already happened or is happening.

I try to look as nonchalant as possible and shrug. "Like I said, I saw him the other day and was just—"

"If you're seeing him, you're in the wrong part of town, Char. Stay away from that guy."

"Why?"

Her gaze is so serious, I can't feel the other pair of eyes on me. Only hers. "He's the Soulless Kings' prez, and he's dangerous."

My jaw drops, but Maggie doesn't seem suspicious of my surprise. The president? What the fuck?

"Just... Stay away from certain parts of town, okay?"

I recover from the shock and give my head a little shake. "How am I supposed to know what parts of town are our territory and which are theirs? So much has changed since I left."

"I'll show you tomorrow." She looks around and shifts the bags to one hand so she can cover her chest with the other. Did bringing up Fender's name make her this uneasy, or can she feel what I feel now?

"Come on, let's go."

We walk the rest of the way to the bikes, and Maggie glances around nervously to keep a lookout for Aunt Annabelle's green Jaguar. Maggie called her a little while ago asking if she'd meet us since we bought too much shit to carry it all home in our saddlebags.

"Where the hell is she?" Maggie mutters.

"It's a big lot. She's probably just taking a minute to find us. Did you tell her what stores we're by?"

Maggie takes out her phone and taps on the screen. She pauses when headlights illuminate us as a vehicle pulls into the lot.

I cover a hand over my eyes to keep myself from being blinded by the SUV's lights, but I still make out the skull wearing a crown on the front plate.

Fuck.

Maggie must recognize who it is too because the phone slips from her hand, and she drops the bags. She carries herself back a few steps. "We need to go," she says to me, just as the doors to the SUV open.

"Why should we run?" I drop my bags and ball my hands into fists like I'm preparing to fight.

"You don't understand," she hisses, backing into her bike and clutching the seat.

Fender, Joker and two guys I don't know walk around the front of the SUV with slow, arrogant strides. Fender leads them, and I don't miss the scowl on his face or the sinister smiles on the others.

Maggie's bike starts up and the engine rattles in my ears, but I don't turn her way.

"Charlotte!"

"I'll catch up with you."

I see Maggie frantically look between me and the rival club members, trying to decide what to do. She waits another few seconds before the bike takes off with a roar. Joker raises the gun in his hand at her, and I almost panic, but Fender raises his hand and waves Joker off. "Let her go. She doesn't matter."

"What do you want, Fender?" I ask, steel in my voice.

I wasn't paranoid. They were his eyes on me, watching me the last few days. There's a tiny ball of hope curled up in my chest at the prospect that maybe it wasn't for malicious reasons, but it dies there when his hardened gray eyes don't flicker with even a hint of humanity.

This isn't about us.

This isn't even about me.

This is about him.

"I think you know what I want."

"To yell at me some more? Maybe talk shit on my old man? I don't even know who you are let alone what you want."

"*Answers*," he sneers, seemingly offended that I didn't already know that.

I feel the blood leave my face when I look between the men and realize what's about to happen and why they're here in that SUV instead of on bikes.

They're going to take me.

They creep closer, Joker easing behind me. My stupid ass pride won't let me move.

"I'll answer whatever the fuck you want me to right here."

Joker laughs and goes to grab my arm, but I anticipate it

and jab my elbow into his sternum. His wheeze fills my ears followed by a grunt by one of the nameless men who I kick in the crotch next. I go to bring my other elbow toward one of the unknowns, but he catches my arm and twists it behind my back until I groan in pain and look up into Fender's stormy eyes. Now they flicker with something, but it's only amusement.

The side of my face explodes as a fist connects with my jaw and white light bursts in my vision. Blood fills my mouth, and I spit it on the ground before turning to see Joker's furious expression and his fist raised like he wants to hit me again.

I turn my gaze to Fender, expecting to see him angry at what Joker just did, but his cold eyes only train on me.

"What the fuck are you going to do?" I mumble, my swelling jaw making it hard to speak.

Fender pulls something from his pocket, and I'm lifted higher to Fender's level. My eyes widen when I see it's a thick needle. He jabs it into my neck and plunges liquid into me that instantly has me feeling dizzy.

"You're right, you know," he says, but it sounds so far away. "You don't know me."

CHAPTER SIX

The dark has a way of making people crazy, feel like they're losing their minds. It has a way of making people talk.

Fender

"This is a mistake, Fender, and you know..."

I glare at Margo, forcing her words to trail off, as I stroll past her toward the office, where church is held. I called an emergency meeting after dumping Charlie in the Nightmare Room—affectionately named because of all the nightmares the Soulless Kings have created for enemies in there—and the voting members have all arrived and are waiting on me.

Margo is likely the only person who would dare to tell me this is a mistake. I ignore the urge to put her in her place because as stubborn as I am and as loyal to my brothers as I am, I'm not certain she's wrong.

When the plan to kidnap Charlie was devised, I'd agreed. Fuck, I'd even ordered the plan to be carried through and plunged the paralytic into her neck. That didn't mean that it had been easy. Especially not when she put up a fight, trying to save herself. The fire Charlie possessed years ago is still there, and while infuriating, it's fucking hot.

"You should have seen that bitch."

Joker's voice registers as I reach the office door, and I stiffen at his words. We aren't even sure she was behind the attack four years ago and my brothers already have her tried, convicted, and sentenced. Why I even give a fuck is beyond me.

Liar. You know exactly why you care.

I shove open the door, and the room immediately goes silent. All eyes turn toward me as I put my weapon in the box to my left, and if I weren't so goddamn pissed, I'd laugh my ass off. There's not a damn thing funny about this situation though. Laughter would just mask the tightly coiled rage slogging through my veins, threatening to burst through the skin and unleash itself into the world.

I take my place at the head of the table and let my gaze roam over each one of my brothers, pausing briefly at each set of eyes. Piston, my VP, bangs the gavel to call church to order and I begin.

"Before we get to the reason for this meeting, is there any other club business that needs discussed?"

Greaser, our Road Captain, stands up, his chair scraping along the hardwood floor as he does. "Bull was late for the exchange last night… again. I charge him extra each time, but the fucker's rich so he doesn't give a shit. I propose we vote on our dealings with him. Either we cut ties or we teach him a lesson, and if he fucks up again, capital punishment."

"Flash, how much money does our deal with Bull bring us in revenue?"

Flash, MC treasurer, scrolls through his laptop, which he brings to every meeting, and then tips his head to the ceiling. We all know this is his way of double checking the computer's math. Flash is smart as hell, and while he advocates for digitizing everything, he never trusts just the machine.

"We make over seventy large. We pay fifteen grand for each shipment and charge Bull cost plus forty percent. It's good money, but with the addition of Infinite Motors, we can afford to lose Bull's business until we find another dealer."

I process this information and nod. "Got it. Let's put it to a vote. All those in favor of cutting ties, thump twice."

No thumps sound on the table, which is our way of voting. I tried the whole 'raise your hand' thing when I was first voted in as president and they all complained that they felt like kindergarten pansies so the 'thump vote' was instituted.

"All those in favor of teaching Bull a lesson, followed by capital punishment if he fails to learn it?"

Every member pounds the table twice with their fists. Unanimous.

"So ordered." Piston bangs the gavel.

I turn my attention to Riker, our Enforcer. "Riker, plan accordingly. I want this dealt with by the end of the day tomorrow."

Riker nods and an evil grin spreads across his face. He's our Enforcer for a reason. Fucker is always spoiling for a fight, and when it's a sanctioned one, he tends to be more vicious. He'll do what needs done, no matter what, but when he has permission to do what he does best, there's no telling what will happen. There isn't anyone I'd rather have in his position, but sometimes he takes things too far which makes it damn hard to clean up after him.

Greaser sits back down, his duty complete.

"Anything else?" When no one else stands, I move on to the reason I called the meeting. "Earlier today, we followed through on the matter voted on yesterday. Charlotte Dorn, daughter of deceased Black Savages' president, Dyno, is being held in the Nightmare Room." I pause to take a deep breath, knowing this next part is going to be difficult, even for a ruthless motherfucker like myself. "We need to discuss and vote on methods of interrogation—"

"We do whatever it takes," Joker barks.

My stare cuts to him, but before I can respond to his statement, Greaser makes his opinion known.

"Prez, she set us up. You're fucking parents were murdered because of her. Why are we even interrogating her? Kill her, bury the body and be done with it."

"We're interrogating her because we agreed that we need answers. Look," I lean forward, bracing my hands on the table in front of me. "If it turns out that everything happened because of her, I'll kill her myself, but we have to be sure. I'm all about revenge and sending a message, but I refuse to murder a woman because of suspicions. That's not how we operate."

"Maybe we should," Riker mumbles.

My head swivels toward him. "You got something to say, say it so everyone can hear. Don't be a fucking pussy about it."

"I said, maybe we should." Riker stands and looks around at our brothers. "We have to send a message to the Black Savages. We've done our best over the last four years, but if that bitch was behind the attack, we can't let that go. Tits or not, she deserves whatever comes her way if she's responsible."

There are murmurs and whispered agreements, but no one has the balls, other than Riker, to challenge me.

"You're all entitled to your opinions, but opinions don't mean shit at this table. We vote, just like we always have." I scan everyone's faces again. "We're not going to get anywhere if we continue to argue about what should happen."

I drop back in my chair and heave out a sigh. I don't know why I even bothered calling this meeting. We all have a common end goal—punish those responsible for the bloodiest ambush on Soulless Kings' property—but the path to get there isn't as clear. I've heard every word that has been said to me since that night, listened to my family bash the woman I thought was meant for me, but it ends now.

Now, we do things right. Get answers. Act accordingly. Nothing more and nothing less.

"Anyone care to start off the suggestions for interrogation?"

"Beating the answers out of her."

"Deprivation... of any kind."

"Waterboarding."

"Drug her."

Answers are shouted out in rapid succession, and I see Curly, our Secretary, furiously scribbling words down in his notebook.

"I submit it for a vote that we do whatever it takes," Joker speaks up.

"All in favor?"

Two thumps all around.

"So ordered."

The bang of the gavel is like a knife to the gut. I don't let it show, but knowing that I just agreed to incredible suffering for Charlie has my stomach in knots. The hatred that's burned in me for four years for that woman had been a constant, a driving force behind my every action. But seeing her, talking to her, even if it wasn't pleasant, changed things. Made me second-guess everything. Because the woman I knew, the woman I fucked, the woman I *loved,* wouldn't have betrayed me. Unless she played me from the beginning. That's what I need to find out.

"I'll take the first shift," I say.

"All due respect, do you think that's wise?" Piston asks. He hates Charlie but he also knows me, and despite the mask I wear, I've never been able to hide my true self from him. He knows every dirty, embarrassing thing about me.

"That's not something that's up for debate," I snap. "Gibson's with her now. I'll relieve him and we'll go down the chain of command for our shifts."

Even though I didn't put anything to a vote, two thumps sound around the table.

"Meeting adjourned."

Piston bangs the gavel one last time, and they all rise to file out of the office, retrieving their weapons from the box as they exit.

"Piston," I call out to him and he turns to face me.

"I didn't want to bring it up in front of everyone else, not yet, but we need to put Trainwreck through his paces."

"Trainwreck?" He looks confused and I think back to if I even told him I'd given the prospect a road name.

"Tyler." Piston recognizes that name and nods. "Little twit was the prospect I took with me for the kidnapping."

"He didn't do well?"

"Let's just say, Trainwreck is an even better road name than I thought it would be." I chuckle as an image surfaces of the expression on his face as we rolled into the mall parking lot earlier today. "Kid has no clue what he's getting into with the Soulless Kings. He's a baby. Turn him into a man. Better yet, turn him into a fucking Soulless King. He either toughens up or he's out. We don't need chicken-shits hanging around, and I certainly don't have the time or the inclination to coddle him through the process."

"Got it." Piston nods and his lips pull up into a grin. "I know it doesn't seem like it, but the kid's had a shit life. He's got what it takes. I'll talk to him."

"We're not fucking head shrinkers. He doesn't need a talking to. He needs to grow a pair and learn. Either he's got it or he doesn't. He's got two weeks to step up or he's out."

"Two weeks isn't much time. Prospects usually have six months to prove themselves."

"We just kidnapped the fucking Black Savages' princess.

That's going to start a goddamn war. I need warriors, not pussies. Two weeks."

I don't stick around to discuss the issue further. Piston doesn't have to agree with me. He just needs to do what he's told.

As I walk through the main room of the clubhouse, I feel Margo's stare searing into the back of my head. I know she has questions about our meeting and she knows she's not going to get answers. Club meetings are closed for a reason, and club business is confidential. She'll no doubt ask Burly for information, but he won't give it.

I descend the steps to the basement, where the Nightmare Room is located. I declared the first shift mine, and now it's time to follow through. Maybe I can convince Charlie to talk, to answer my questions, and this can all end, one way or another. I order Gibson to leave his post and he does, without hesitation.

As I step up to the monitors that are mounted on the wall to the right of the door, shock that I finally have her, *here*, settles in.

The room is kept dark as a way to enforce sensory deprivation. The dark has a way of making people crazy, feel like they're losing their minds. It has a way of making people talk. The paralytic seems to have worn off, and I'm able to see Charlie because of the infrared cameras that are installed. She's sitting in a corner, too close to the door for my liking, with her hands wrapped around her knees.

I put my finger over the button for the speaker inside the room and take a deep breath to steady myself and to prepare to inject as much authority into my tone as possible.

I'm going to need to summon all the strength I can for what I'm about to do.

CHAPTER SEVEN

If words produced a physical feeling, those six would mimic a punch to the solar plexus.

Charlie

"Move to another corner."

My eyes snap up to where I hear his voice, and it takes me a moment to realize it isn't coming from him. It's coming from a speaker. Whatever the fuck he jabbed into my neck seems to have worn off. I haven't decided if that's good or not.

On one hand, if I were still out of it, I wouldn't give a damn about where I am. But as it stands, I am fully aware of the blackness swallowing me up and the dire situation I've seemed to have gotten myself into. My cheek throbs from the punch I took earlier, and it serves as a reminder that Fender isn't going to protect me... Maybe not even from himself.

It's freezing in here, but with the knowledge that he can somehow see me in the dark, I stiffen my muscles to stop shivering and push myself up off the floor. I square my shoulders and move my head around to uselessly search for a camera even though I can't see a damn thing.

"Move to another corner." Fender's deep baritone raises the hairs on the back of my neck, and I clench my jaw and stand in place.

A faint noise sounds only a few feet away, a click and a whoosh and then another click. I realize too late it was the door. No light filtered into the room when it opened, so I assume it's pitch black outside this place, too. Wherever 'this place' is.

"Why the fuck do you have to be so stubborn?" he growls, his voice close. His footsteps echo on the floor as he comes closer.

"You used to like that about me."

Fender chuckles but there's no humor in it. In fact, in the dark, it's sinister and scary. Not that I'd ever admit to that. Being scared is weak, and if there's anything my dad taught me, it's how to *not* be weak.

"Don't mistake what we had for liking anything about you other than what's between your legs."

My chest constricts, but I don't let the hurt show on my face even when I know he can't see me anymore.

Fuck you too, Fender.

I blink against the darkness and shift along the wall to put more distance between us. The coldness of the concrete seeps through my long-sleeve T-shirt.

"If you wanted to catch up, we could've done it over a cup of coffee. Or, I know," Sarcasm drips from my tone as I snap my fingers, like my next words are the culmination of a brilliant mind at work. "You could've called me. You know, like a normal person."

More footsteps coming toward me. I wouldn't need to hear them to know when he's close because the air around my head seems to disappear. My heartbeat thuds an erratic rhythm in my ears, and when I feel his calloused hands brush both of my arms, I can't stop the reflexive jerk of my body.

"Jumpy?"

Fender's breath teases my cheek as he whispers in my ear. I turn in the opposite direction of his voice, intent on walking away from him, but his hands move to box me in. I pull my bottom lip between my teeth, and seconds tick by before the metallic taste of blood reaches my tongue.

"We can do this one of two ways." His voice is louder and seems to bounce off the wall behind me and echo around my head. "The easy way... I ask questions, you answer. I like the answers, you're home in time for breakfast with the fam."

"And the second option?"

"The hard way." He leans into me so that the hard wall of his chest grazes against my nipples through our clothes. Or my clothes. He could be naked for all I know. "Which I gotta say, I'm not opposed to." He presses his hips against me, the evidence of what this is doing to him hitting me in the stomach.

This is getting him off. Having me here in a dark, cold room is getting him off. I shouldn't be surprised considering what our sex life *used* to look like, but I am. What am I even here for? He wants to ask me questions so... information on Black Savages?

Yes. That's exactly what this is. I'm back for two seconds and already he wants me to betray my family. Again.

Over my dead body.

"Let me get this straight," I say, unable to keep the words from passing my lips. "I can either answer your questions or you're gonna fuck them outta me?"

I don't believe my own words. I don't know who Fender is anymore, but I know he isn't a rapist. He's bluffing, and there's nothing I love more than calling someone's bluff.

I slide my hand under his shirt, and my lips twitch as he tenses beneath my touch. I move my hand to the waistband of his pants and tuck my fingers inside while I run my other hand over his chest. "Is this what you think I'm afraid of?"

"Stop," he growls, although it's hard to tell if he's serious by the heat in his tone.

I have an effect on him. Still, after all this time.

Good to know.

I tuck my hand further into his pants until my fingertips graze his bulge.

"I said, stop."

Fender grabs my arm and runs his hand along it until he reaches the wrist just above his waistband. He wraps his fingers around it and yanks it out of his pants and up above my head. His grip is hard, but I ignore the pain. His breathing is ragged, and I bite my lip when I realize my breathing is rough as well.

Fuck.

Even though I can't see him, I feel the moment he pushes away from the wall, away from me. If it weren't for the thump of his boots on the floor, the room would be silent.

I squint, trying to find him in the darkness, but it's as useless this time as it had been the other hundred times I tried. I'm struggling to stay still, stay against the wall, but I really don't feel like colliding with him so I do. I lean my head back slowly and point my eyes toward the ceiling.

I count his steps as if they're seconds, but he doesn't pace for much longer. Based on the feeling of suffocation, he's stopped in front of me again. I take a deep breath and hold it, waiting for him to make the next move.

"Why, Charlotte?" His breath whooshes out of him when he speaks. "Why'd you do it?"

My eyebrows knit. "Do what?"

"You know what," he grits out, and it sounds like his teeth are clenched. His fists are probably clenched at his sides, too.

"Fen—"

"I told you not to call me that!"

"What the fuck am I supposed to call you then? I can't call

you Chris, and I can't call you Fender." My anger rises as I shout the words. "I'd call you 'asshole', but something tells me you wouldn't approve of that either."

Silence engulfs me. My chest is heaving, and my heart is racing. Suddenly, there's a blinding light in my eyes, and I have to blink several times to adjust to it. When I do, I make out the cell phone in Fender's hand just to the side of my head. He's shining the light on me, but I'm able to see his face in the shadows. A shiver races up my spine at the murderous rage etched in his expression.

"Answer the fucking question," he demands.

"Get the light out of my eyes and I will," I shout.

Fender glares at me for a few seconds before he lowers his phone. He doesn't turn the light off, but rather he uses it to guide himself to the door. I try to take in my surroundings, what I'm able to see. There's what looks like an electrical panel next to the door.

I watch as Fender punches in a code, and after a series of beeps, the panel door pops open, revealing what I assume is some high-tech shit. Soulless Kings always had fancier shit than us. The glow of his cell isn't bright enough to make out details, but he taps his finger on whatever the panel is hiding and a screen lights up in front of him, casting a little more light.

Fender taps the screen a few more times, and the room is bathed in light, allowing me my first glimpse of the walls surrounding me and the man who put me here. The room is stark, empty, cold. The man is coiled tighter than a snake about to strike, and his already buff muscles flex over his sleeves, reminding me how much he's grown since I last saw him. He's wearing jeans, a T-shirt, and his cut. The crown-wearing skull seems to mock me from the worn leather.

When Fender turns around, he stalks toward me with purpose, a storm brewing in his gray eyes. He stops just in front of me, his stare never wavering. He's standing tall, his shoulders squared, his jaw granite hard and wrinkles creasing his forehead.

I resist the urge to reach out and smooth away the wrinkles. I need to remember that neither of us are the people from four years ago, and my touch isn't welcome.

"I'm only gonna ask one more time." Fender takes a deep breath, exhales it slowly. "Why. Did. You. Do. It?"

I sigh and close my eyes against the headache that's already forming from my eyes struggling to adjust to the light. I don't know when the questions about Black Savages are coming, but it seems right that we get this one out of the way. I won't be answering any others.

"I left because you told me to. I assumed after that night... I didn't think you'd want to see me anymore because of who I am."

"So you admit to it?" His eyes narrow like he's skeptical.

"Admit to what?"

"Goddamnit," he roars and his movement is so swift, I don't have time to register it until his fist is wrapped around strands of my hair, and he's pulling my head back. "You're not this fucking stupid, Charlie."

I wince at the nickname. Fender is the one who gave it to me, the only person who uses it. To everyone else, I'm Charlotte or Char and sometimes even princess, but Charlie? That's reserved for only him.

"What the fuck are you talking about?"

"That night?" Something flashes in his expression, and for a moment, I think it's pain, but he masks it so fast it's hard to tell. "Why did you set me up?"

If words produced a physical feeling, those six would mimic a punch to the solar plexus. Is that what he thinks? That I had something to do with the attack, the bloodshed that took his parents from him? I knew he hated me because

I was one of them. I *understood* why he hated me. But how could he believe I was a part of that?

My eyes slide closed as memories of that night barrel into my brain like a speeding freight train. I hadn't witnessed most of it, at least not while it was happening, and so much of it is a blur. What I do remember, with unambiguous clarity, is putting a bullet in Sharp, a Black Savages Sergeant at Arms, and saving Fender from the same fate. I remember the fear that had latched onto my soul, knowing that punishment would be severe if my family found out about what I'd done. I remember being shouted at to leave, and I remember Fender not having my back.

What I absolutely *do not* remember, is having anything to do with the Soulless Kings' death toll. I force my eyes open to see that Fender is still staring at me, waiting. He wants answers, but will he believe me? Or is he so convinced of my guilt that it doesn't matter what I say?

"How could you believe I had something to do with that?"

He glances away like he can't even look at me, and my stomach barrels to the floor. There's so much heartache etched into his expression that I can't help remember that I wasn't there to comfort him. I wasn't there to get him through it. And he hates me so much he's choosing not to be there for me while I'm going through my own father's death. He's choosing to blame me for all of his struggles instead. Or at least he's trying to.

He's a bastard for this. For bringing me here and for questioning me like I'd ever do something like that. Still, staring at him now, I can see the old Fender. I fucking miss him.

I take a deep breath and reach up to ease his hold on my hair. Surprisingly, he allows it and releases the locks. He turns his gaze to me. I rub the sore spot on my scalp but am careful to not break eye contact. Fender's nostrils flare, and when I stand up on my tiptoes, he sucks in a breath.

Leaning forward, slowly, tentatively, and fully aware that this could blow up in my face any second, I touch my lips to his.

CHAPTER EIGHT

Now I don't know what love is anymore, only hate exists in my world. But one thing is certain: If Charlie keeps kissing me like that, I'm liable to forget what hate is, too.

Fender

Charlie's mouth is colder than I remember but just as soft. I don't kiss her back, and when her tongue slides across the seam of my lips, it's enough to jolt me out of my stupor.

"Ain't happenin' babe," I say after gripping her arms and forcing her away from me.

Hurt flashes in her green irises, and I force myself to ignore it. I approved her kidnapping because I want answers, and I'll be damned if I'm going to let her mouth, her body, *her*, tempt me away from that. Eyes on the prize and all that shit.

"Just answer the question, Charlie." I sigh, the weight of the last four years crashing over me in waves.

Charlie crosses her arms over her chest, and I have to turn away from the sight of her T-shirt stretching across her tits. I walk to the opposite wall and brace my fists against it, hanging my head and taking several deep breaths to cool the lust threatening to take over.

"I have a question of my own."

Her voice is low, almost as if she's afraid to speak. I let my arms fall to my sides and turn back around to face her, my brow arching as if to say 'spit it out'.

"What makes you think I had something to do with it?"

I hate to admit it, but that's a damn good question. The thought that she could do that, that she could orchestrate that level of violence never would have crossed my mind if the seed hadn't been planted by my brothers. But it *had* been planted and it's grown like a fucking weed, overtaking my existence until there's no room for anything good.

I let my gaze roam her body from head to toe while I mull over my response, enjoying the way she seems to squirm under my scrutiny. If I let myself, I could get lost in her sex-appeal. I return my attention to her face and force the walls I've built to shift back into place.

"How could I not think that?" I thread my fingers through my hair in frustration. "You were born to be my enemy. Am I really supposed to believe you had nothing to do with it? That you were with me because you had real feelings for me?" Her eyes widen as I speak, but I don't let that stop me. "C'mon, Charlie, do you really think *I'm* that fucking stupid?"

Her mouth opens and closes several times, but no words come out. She swallows, the action visible in the column of her slender neck. A neck that used to be a sexy as fuck display of my mark, my claim on her. Now it's like a blank canvas, clean, fresh, new, and I hate the urge to dirty it up that slithers through me.

"I don't know what you want from me." She shrugs but then does something so reminiscent of the old Charlie. She straightens her spine and squares her shoulders, her MC princess persona like a second skin that she wears with pride.

"I had nothing to do with what happened. Fucking *nothing*! That doesn't matter though, does it? You already have your mind made up, so my words don't mean shit to you."

"That's not true," I argue.

Liar. You're just as guilty as being judge and jury as your brothers.

"Dammit, Fender, it is and you know it. Your brothers have your brain so warped that no matter what I say, you're not going to believe me. Unless, of course, I tell you I *did* plan it. That I betrayed you, set you up and burned your world to the fucking ground."

My tenuous hold on control snaps like a rubber band that's stretched too far. I advance on her and push her backward until she hits the wall, pinning her there with my weight, my face inches from hers.

"You don't get to talk about my brothers," I sneer. "You don't get to sling accusations at the Soulless Kings and get away with it. Not after what you did."

She attempts to shove me away from her, but she's a pint-sized pixie and I don't budge. Her physical strength has never matched the fire in her temper, and this is a perfect example of that.

"Ya know what?" she asks, the attitude seeming to fizzle out through her slumping shoulders. "Forget it. You don't believe me, fine. Just do whatever it is you're gonna do to punish me. It certainly can't be any worse than what I'll face at the hands of the Black Savages when they learn the truth."

The resignation in her tone sets off an emotion in me that I haven't felt in a long time, that I haven't allowed myself to feel. Being sad is weak. Being sad gets people like me killed. Being sad is a luxury that a Soulless King isn't granted. I take several steps back as if to physically distance myself from the feeling.

C'mon Fen, don't let her do this to you. You're better than this. Stronger.

The problem is, apparently I'm not. Not when it comes to Charlie. I shove the emotion into my vault and do my best to ignore the way her eyes appear dimmer, like her life essence is slowly dwindling away to nothing.

"You say you had nothing to do with it. Everyone else says otherwise." I pull my cell phone out of my pocket and glance at the time before folding my arms across my chest and widening my stance. "You've got four minutes to convince me that you're telling the truth. One minute for each year you were gone. After that, my shift is over, and if I still don't believe you, maybe Piston can get some answers."

Her eyes widen for a brief moment before she narrows them and shoots daggers at me.

That's better. Fight me, Charlie. I welcome it.

"I don't know how to convince someone who doesn't really want to be convinced."

"C'mon. You fucking sank your teeth into me when you were doing Black Savages' dirty work. Gotta say, you had me convinced then."

I'm baiting her, taunting her. There isn't much she can do to prove her innocence. I *want* her to be innocent, I *want* her to be the girl I loved, I *want* to be the man I was before that night. But we don't always get what we want. And on the off chance that I'm wrong, that there is some way she can earn my trust back, I'm willing to give her a few minutes to try.

"I loved you, you idiot!"

"*Bullshit*. You fucking used me."

She runs her hands over her face like I've exhausted her, and when she lets them fall to her sides, her mouth opens and closes like she wants to say something but can't. Or she can't find the words.

I stand there, waiting, watching her eyes dart back and forth between me and the door. Before I know what's happening, she's advancing on me. When she's mere inches from my body, she jumps and instinctively, I catch her.

Her mouth crashes down on mine as her legs wrap around my waist. I grab her ass and carry her back to the wall, trapping her between my now throbbing boner and the cold concrete. I brace my hands on either side of her head and lean into the kiss.

Charlie moans when I thrust my tongue past her lips and tangle it with hers. I'm blinded by the rush of heat she's ignited in me, all hatred and anger gone as I give in to what she's offering. I grind my pelvis against her, and the friction has me moaning just as loud as her.

"Gotta say, when we said we'd do whatever it takes, I'm pretty damn sure this isn't what we fucking had in mind."

I freeze at the intrusion, my mouth still fused to Charlie's. Our eyes are now open, and we're looking at each other like teenagers who just got busted by the teacher for making out behind the bleachers in the gym.

"I'm gonna assume you now know for a fact that she had nothing to do with that night... *prez.*"

I lower Charlie to the floor and take a step back. After a few deep breaths, I turn around and face Piston. His eyes automatically lower to the bulge in my pants and when he returns his gaze to my face, his eyebrows are raised. He's lucky that he's more than just a brother, my VP. He's my best friend and that's the *only* thing that's keeping me from beating the shit out of him for the way he just spoke to me.

"Don't you dare talk to me that way," I growl. He may get to keep breathing but he'll damn sure know he's crossed a line. "I'll do whatever the fuck I want, whenever I want, however I want. And if I want to use her like she used me, I'll fucking do it."

Piston narrows his eyes with suspicion. He sees through my bullshit statement about using her. I've never been able to fool him about anything and that's usually a good thing. Not this time, though.

He stalks toward Charlie, and it takes everything in me

not to react. When he reaches her, he doesn't touch her, but he does get in her face.

"You fucking bitch. I gotta hand it to you." He huffs out an evil laugh. "In under an hour, you've managed to once again sink your claws into him. You must have some premium pussy. Maybe I—"

The crack of her palm on Piston's cheek echoes in the room. I'm shocked at her action, but I shouldn't be. She's a Black Savage after all. My little pint-sized pixie is back, and she's not taking shit from anyone.

"You've got a lot of nerve—"

"Stop." The word tears out of me with so much force that if the Nightmare Room weren't so solidly built, the walls would crumble.

Piston whirls on me, shock written on his face, while Charlie doesn't move a muscle, doesn't react.

"That's enough." I walk toward the door. "Piston, let's go. You can have your turn later."

"You're just gonna let her get away with that?"

You're damn right I'm going to let her get away with that. At least for now. While I clear my head and re-evaluate what the hell we're doing.

That's not what comes out of my mouth though.

"No," I respond, shaking my head. "I'm punishing her."

I open the panel that houses the control for the room and turn off the light. Once the darkness hides both of them from my view, I hear Piston's footsteps as he comes toward me. I then tap the screen, from memory, to open the door. Piston and I exit into the hallway, him sporting a sinister grin and me sporting a goddamn headache.

As Piston starts to chatter on and on about what he plans to do to her when he starts his shift, my mind wanders and I tune him out. I thought I knew what happened. I thought that there was nothing Charlie could do to tip the scales in her favor.

Then she kissed me. One fucking kiss and every illusion I'd held on to for the last four years had shattered.

I'm transported back to square one with no idea what the hell is going on and zero clue how to fix that. I loved Charlie then. I believed she loved me. Now I don't know what love is anymore, only hate exists in my world. But one thing is certain: if Charlie keeps kissing me like that, I'm liable to forget what hate is, too.

CHAPTER NINE

I wonder what I would've done if I had known who he was before he staked his claim on my heart.

Charlie

$\mathcal{I}$ don't know how much time has passed since Fender left, but I know it's been a while. I stood in what I think is the middle of the room with my arms crossed over my chest until my legs burned and my knees started to buckle. I didn't want to cower in a corner.

Now I'm sitting next to the door, leaned back against the wall with my legs stretched out in front of me. I can't keep from shivering anymore, but I make up for it by glaring at the ceiling. I don't know where the camera is, but I hope my eyes are pointed at it.

I'm pissed. So fucking infuriated, I hope he never comes back just so I can smite him by starving while I glare at the ceiling, hating him until the end.

Or at least I wish I hated him.

His words play in my mind and they slice through everything I've ever known.

I'm punishing her.

You'll have your turn later.

Like I'm some toy he can pawn off to his friends. Fuck him and fuck his punishments. Fuck his vulnerability. Fuck his pain. Fuck it all.

"You're a bastard!" I yell, pretending what I'm looking at really is the camera.

I don't expect an answer, so I'm surprised when a voice booms from the speaker which is above my head. It isn't Fender's. "You have five seconds to move away from the door. If you choose not to, you'll be shot with a stun gun as soon as the door opens."

"Who are you?"

"Five. Four. Three…"

I turn my head toward the door and debate on whether I should try to run or not. No? We're on an MC club's property as far as I can tell. I'm not an idiot. They guard their fences just as much as we guard ours.

Am I even a part of that 'we'?

"Last chance," the voice says.

I can't move, even though I know how stupid that decision is. I move, they win. I do what they say, they win.

I cross one ankle over the other and lift my middle finger into the air.

The room suddenly brightens, and I close my eyes against it, unable to adjust.

The latch clicks and the door opens. I have my hand shielding my eyes from the light, and I'm not even standing, but the man holds true to his promise, and a jolt of electricity rocks my body. My arms shoot by my sides, and my head knocks into the wall, but I only register the noise from it. I can't feel anything but the voltage pulsing through me.

It stops after a minute, and I gasp for breath. I yank the clamps that are dug into my side off me and scramble back away from the door.

I'm still catching my breath and running my hands over my body as if to brush the shock away. Shit, that hurt.

The door is pushed open further and Fender's best friend, even back then, appears with a grin.

Piston.

"There," he says, a shit-eating grin on his face. "Now we're even."

The handprint I put on his face earlier is long gone while I'm pretty sure I'll be feeling the effects of that shock for at least a day. I wouldn't call that even.

"Is it your turn to *play?*" I sneer, eyeing the chair he drags in behind him.

He closes the door behind him and places the chair in the center of the room. "Sit."

"No."

He raises a brow. "Did you already forget that I'm not as nice as Fender?" He glances at the stun gun now secured at his hip.

I stare at him and ball my fists at my sides. "What is it that you want, Piston? To know if I had something to do with the raid on Soulless Kings? No, I didn't. It's been four years, so if you haven't been able to figure that out by now, you must not be as smart as you think you are."

"Maybe it isn't all about that. Maybe it benefits us to have the little Black Savages' princess at our disposal, have you considered that?"

Yes, I have considered that. Kidnapping an MC princess is a hell of a way to send a message, and it's also a surefire way to start a war. But they're missing something. I'm the princess who left the castle. I abandoned my family. As much as I know they'll raise hell to come get me, it's only out of loyalty. I'm pretty certain most of the Black Savages couldn't give a fuck about what happens to me.

He nods to the chair. "Let's go."

"Why?"

"Because I said so." His face is hard as stone, and I can see how much he hates me right now. I can feel it filling the room, making it hard to breathe.

He puts his hand on the stun gun, and I lift myself to my feet. I don't take my eyes off him as I walk to the chair and sit. I give him the same dead look he's giving me and hope it sends the message that the feeling is mutual. I remember liking Piston. He made me laugh, he was always so nice to me. Now he looks like he's changed as much as Fender has.

He secures my wrists to the arms of the chair and then my ankles to the legs.

When he's done, he stands up straight and stares down at me. The hate in his eyes is still there, but they flicker with something else so fast I almost miss it.

Pain. He had people die that day too.

"I'm gonna ask you a few questions, and you're going to be honest with me. If you're not, there will be consequences. I'll be able to tell if you're lying."

"How will you be able to tell? Because they aren't the answers you want? You're looking for someone to blame, Piston, and—"

A cracking sound echoes off the walls when the back of his hand connects with my cheek, and my head whips to the side. I bit my tongue when he hit me, so blood now coats it.

"The only things I want to hear coming out of your mouth are the answers to my questions, is that understood?"

Answers you won't accept.

I spit blood on the floor and clench my eyes shut with the migraine that seems to be getting worse every time someone comes in here. Piston doesn't wait for me to respond before he dives in.

"Did you know about the attack on Soulless Kings before it occurred?"

"No."

"No," he echoes. He shakes his head, already pissed.

"You're the daughter of our rivals' MC president, and you didn't know about a war they planned to wage."

"I *was* the daughter of the MC president." My voice comes out as a sneer, but my eyes burn from the memory of my father's funeral. "There's a new president now."

He smacks me across the face again, this time using his other hand, and I whip in the opposite direction I was facing. My breaths are coming heavier, and I grip the edge of the chair's arms, digging my nails into the wood.

"That wasn't an answer to my question."

"You didn't ask a question!"

He grips my jaw and forces me back to look at him. "Did you know about the raid before it happened?"

"No!"

"Did you know Black Savages were planning a war?"

I jerk out of his grasp. "No, I didn't. I didn't know anything."

"And you expect us to believe that?"

"No." I spit more blood onto the floor, splattering Piston's boot. "I expected Fender to believe it, but never you. Never your club."

"Why? Because you fucked him? You never meant anything to him, Charlotte."

My ears are ringing, but it doesn't drown out Piston's words playing on repeat in my mind. They're similar to Fender's.

Don't mistake what we had for liking anything about you other than what's between your legs.

I let my head fall forward some and stare at a patch on Piston's cut. It's the Soulless Kings' symbol and one I remember seeing so clearly for the first time inked into Fender's chest. It was how I found out he was a member of a rival club. He hid his cut from me, but he couldn't hide his ink. Not forever.

I wonder what I would've done if I had known who he

was before he staked his claim on my heart. Would I have still fallen in love with him? At the time, it didn't feel like I had a choice.

"You're right," I whisper, not really even talking to Piston. "I never meant anything to him."

I peer up and look into Piston's eyes after getting the admission out. It wasn't for Piston, but this is.

"But he meant everything to me. I didn't set him up, and I would've told him if I knew something was going to happen. I would've betrayed my family for him, just like I ended up doing anyway. I killed one of my own to protect him."

Piston's face is still hard, but his eyes have softened some.

"But you know what?" I ask, a humorless laugh crawling up my throat. "I regret it. I should've never betrayed my family for you people, or even for him."

That seems to piss him off, and he lifts his hand to hit me again. He pauses when his phone beeps, and he pulls it from his pocket and stares at the screen for a moment before piercing me with a glare.

He turns and walks to the door, beeping coming from the panel he presses. Soon he's gone, and the light turns off, basking me in darkness yet again.

CHAPTER TEN

Did he just give me the answer to all my questions, the antidote to all my fears?

Fender

"We're doing this now?"

Piston strides through the door and off the small cement slab that sits at the front of the clubhouse. I catch sight of the stun gun at his hip and the spatter of blood on the back of his hand. My gut twists into knots, but I force it to unravel and focus on the task at hand. I'll get an update from Piston later. Right now, I need to focus. *We* need to focus.

"Riker doesn't fuck around."

Riker has a contact that works for Bull and just got word that Bull is making a buy from another supplier. It's the perfect opportunity to send him a message and take out the competition. Where the meet is set is on Soulless Kings' territory and anyone who dares to conduct their business where they don't belong deserves what's coming to them.

Piston cracks his knuckles before pulling the gun he keeps stashed at the small of his back and checking the clip. He does all of this as we walk, and when we reach the others and our bikes, he bends to do the same with the gun in his boot. Knowing Piston, he's probably got a few knives hidden somewhere and there will be a third gun in his saddlebags, maybe a fourth.

Riker's straddling his bike, the engine running, and he's wearing a huge grin which tells me he's out for blood. He's always out for blood. Joker's next to him, and he's playing with his butterfly knife while he waits.

"What's the plan?" I ask as I mount my own bike.

"This is gonna be like a Sunday stroll through the park that them highfalutin people take," Riker responds. "We crash the buy, take out the competition, and Bull gets the message. Pretty standard run, prez."

"Any idea who he's meeting with?" It doesn't really matter in the grand scheme of things, but I'm curious.

"Nah, my contact didn't know. He's pretty low level in Bull's crew, so he got me what he could. We're heading south, to the abandoned warehouse at the edge of town."

I nod and then check my own weapons. This is the perfect distraction from the little problem sitting in our basement. Sure, they could handle this Bull situation without me, but I need to get the fuck away from this place, away from her.

"Let's ride," I shout.

As president, I'm in the lead position, with Piston to my right and Riker to my left. Joker, Gibson, Craze, Pony, Chaser and Trainwreck are following. When we clear the Soulless Kings' property line and leave the dirt roads behind, we pick up speed and fly down the asphalt.

The view of the Pacific Ocean fuels me as it always does when I cruise the Coastal Highway. I've spent hours, hell probably days, driving up and down the coast throughout my lifetime. It centers me, makes me feel like I'm a part of something bigger than our little corner of the world.

When we near the turnoff for the warehouse, the hairs on

the back of my neck stand up. I glance to my right, then my left, and notice that Piston and Riker's shoulders are a little straighter and scowls scrunch their faces. They feel it too. Someone is watching us. This isn't going to be a Sunday stroll in the fucking park.

We all pull into the lot and park our bikes next to the big black Suburban. The SUV is a joke. Everywhere you'd normally see chrome, there's gold. Flashy, ugly, arrogant gold. It's Bull's way of showing off his money. I'm tempted to smash out the windows and destroy his custom rims, but I hold myself back. If I do that, they'll know we're here.

I'm the first to dismount and the others follow suit. We each double check our weapons, and my eyebrows raise to my hairline when I see Trainwreck pull a sawed-off shotgun from his saddlebags and what appears to be a mini handgrenade out of his pocket. He kisses the hand-grenade, as if for luck, and shoves it back in his pocket. Holy fuck, this kid isn't playing around.

"You see that?" Piston leans in and whispers as he tips his head in Trainwreck's direction.

"Yeah, I fucking saw," I growl. "This isn't the time or place, but I'll be having a conversation with the kid later."

Piston chuckles and steps away from me. We gather in a circle, and I give Riker the go-ahead to run things down one last time. He talks for a few minutes, and it's hard to miss the excitement in his voice. Violence… it's what he lives for.

"Okay, are we ready?" Riker takes a moment to look into each set of eyes.

"Uh, one question," Trainwreck speaks up. He glances around nervously, and his Adam's apple bobs as he swallows. This is not a man—a goddamn kid—who needs to be carrying the weapons he is. "Where's the other supplier?"

I glare at him and he ducks his head but only for a moment. He lifts it and stares me directly in the eyes, and his face is hard.

"I can't be the only person who's wondering this." He looks from one brother to the next. "Seriously? No one else thinks it's suspicious that the only vehicle here is Bull's?" He glances around the surrounding empty lot as if to emphasize his point.

Well, shit. Maybe he isn't as dumb as I thought. I have no doubt we'd all been wondering the same thing, but Trainwreck is a fucking prospect so he doesn't get to question anything.

"Doesn't fucking matter, *prospect*," Riker sneers, reminding him of his place. "We're here. We go in, get the job done, and get the fuck out. End of discussion."

Murmurs of agreement fill the air, and we move to the entrance. We aren't quiet about it either. Why would we be? We want our enemy to know we're coming. We want them to wonder 'who's out there'. We want them to be scared. We want them to quake in their shoes and piss their pants. And the louder we are, the more fear they'll feel.

When we round the corner at the opposite end of the old production floor, two men are at the end of the hallway, guns drawn and pointing in our direction. Good. They heard us. They're scared.

Recognition flares as we stare them down. "Sonofabitch," I mumble under my breath.

"What's up, prez?"

"What is it?"

Piston and Riker speak at the same time. The tension emanating off of them is palpable, and I have to wonder if they really don't know. The bandana-wearing skull patch should have been a dead giveaway. Not to mention the black bandanas covering the heads of the gun-toting dickwads.

"Fucking Black Savages."

"Well, well, well, what do we have here?" Bull says as he comes around the corner that's beyond Brick and Arrow, the two Black Savage fucks in front of me.

"Late as always, I see," Riker taunts Bull. "Good to know the Soulless Kings aren't the only ones you're willing to fuck over." Bull bristles but says nothing. "You do realize though, that this is our territory and those yahoos," he tilts his head toward Brick and Arrow, "represent our biggest rivals?"

"Couldn't help but notice that there were no bikes in the parking lot when we rolled up," Joker adds his two cents from behind me. "What'd ya do? Have mommy drop you off for your play date?"

Our crew laughs at the joke, but no one else thinks it's funny. Both Brick and Arrow pull back the hammer on their guns, readying themselves to take us out. Idiots. We may not look like it, but we're armed to the teeth. They won't get more than one shot off before we spill their blood all over the floor.

"Why are you here?" Bull asks in an attempt to redirect the attention back to him.

"You mean besides to have a *conversation* with you?" Riker challenges.

"No, I mean, how'd you even know I'd be here?" Bull pauses for a second. "And that other thing. The conversation thing."

"You're not very thorough in your background checks, are ya?" Riker will not mention his contact, but he will let Bull speculate.

"What's he talking about?" Arrow turns his head to Bull and glares at him.

"I have no idea. He's just trying to scare me." Bull's tone is not confident, but he knows that the Black Savages are just as ruthless as we are, so he's scrambling. "Everyone that works for me has been vetted. There are no holes in my system. I swear."

"See, Bull, that's the thing." Riker takes a step forward. "You're so focused on shit that doesn't even matter that you're missing what's right in front of your fat little face."

"What? What am I missing?"

I step forward to join Riker and inject as much malice into my tone as I possibly can. "You're now caught between both sides of the deadliest rivals in the state." I glance over my shoulder at my brothers and give a terse nod. All of them raise their weapons and get them cocked and ready. When I return my attention to Bull, a grin is tugging my lips. This is gonna be fun. "We were just going to show up here today, rough you up a bit, teach you a lesson, and then continue with business as usual. But now? I'm not feeling the least bit fucking generous."

Five seconds after I stop talking, my brothers open fire. Every bullet penetrates their singular target: Bull. With each hit, his body jerks, and when the gunfire ceases, he falls to the floor, a pool of blood flowing from beneath him.

While they'd focused on Bull, I'd squeezed my trigger and put a slug in both arms of Brick and Arrow. Their guns are now lying at their feet and they're shouting out their pain. I stalk toward them, signaling Riker to follow.

When we reach them, I grab Brick and slam him against the wall. Riker does the same with Arrow. Both continue to wail and whine. It's pathetic and there's no way in hell they ever would've been patched members of the Soulless Kings.

Fucking pussies.

"I'm gonna give you both a chance to walk outta here. But only one." My tone is hard, my body rigid with rage, as I growl in Brick's face. "You two were out here, acting as guards when we got here, and that tells me that you weren't the ones sealing the deal with dead man over there." I tilt my head in the direction of Bull's bloody carcass. "Who else is here?"

"Fuck you," Brick says through clenched teeth.

"Wow, you really are that stupid."

I grip the butt of my gun and pull it out from where I'd tucked it back into my waistband. I shove the barrel into

Brick's thigh and squeeze the trigger. He hollers out in agony as he slides to the floor. I could kill him, but I need one of these fucks alive to take a message back to their club.

"You gonna be that dumb?" Riker asks behind me.

"Black Savages don't negotiate wi—"

A gunshot echoes around me, and I hear Arrow's shout before he falls to the ground, clutching the fresh bullet hole in his thigh. Riker and I stare at both of them in disgust for a brief moment, watching them whimper on the concrete, before we head back to the rest of our crew.

A slow clapping sounds from behind me, punctuated by heavy boots hitting concrete.

I whirl around and standing there, smug as can be, is Leal, another fucking Black Savages member. The patch on his cut catches my eye, and I take a moment to read the rocker under the skull: President.

Well, shit.

"So you're the shit for brains who's trying to steal our business."

Leal quirks a brow. "And you're the motherfucker who fell for it."

"What're you talking about?" Piston demands as he comes to stand next to me.

"Do you really think I need to poach your customers?" Leal crosses his arms over his chest. "I set you up. Bull was a means to an end, that's all."

"What 'end'?" I demand.

"I believe you have something of mine."

Tension coils my muscles, and I can practically feel it rolling off of Piston.

Charlie.

"You've got forty-eight hours to drop her at the east entrance to Black Savages' property. You don't and we'll have a repeat performance of four years ago."

"What makes you think we won't just go back and

prepare for war? Gotta say, I'm not quite ready to give her up yet."

"And that's exactly what will get you killed, just like your parents." Leal takes a step closer to me, and I point my gun at him. "Charlotte is a Black Savage. You're a Soulless King. As long as you keep her, you're jeopardizing the lives of every member of your club."

I can't help the growl that crawls up my throat and passes my lips. I could kill Leal, right here, right now, but he's causing more questions to flow through my mind, and I want answers.

"Still think I'm gonna pass. I'm liking our fucking odds."

Leal shrugs. "Your choice. But know this… when we attack, we'll have one more soldier on our side. She may have been clueless then, but her eyes will be wide fucking open this time."

With that statement, Leal shouts at Brick and Arrow to 'get up' before he turns and walks away. His men limp behind him, bitching with each step they take. When they're out of sight, I glance at Piston before shifting my focus to the others.

"Clean this shit up," I order, pointing at Bull.

I shove my way past them as they all get to work. My boots echo as I walk through the empty warehouse, and when I push through the entrance, I realize it's gotten late.

Leal's words roll around in my head. What did he mean when he said 'she may have been clueless then'? Did he just give me the answer to all my questions, the antidote to all my fears? I'm so lost in my head, I don't hear the door open behind me or register that I'm not alone until Piston steps up to my right.

"So…" Piston rocks back on his heels and shoves his hands in his pockets.

"What?" I snap. I don't feel like hearing his usual shit. Not now.

"Are you thinking what I'm thinking?"

"Jesus, spit it the fuck out." I glare at him and I'm sure he sees it, even in the dark.

"Shit, Fen, have we all been wrong? This whole time did we get it wrong?"

"Yeah." I take a deep breath, hold it for a few seconds before letting it whoosh out of me. "Yeah, I think we did."

I stride away from Piston and mount my bike. I need to get out of here, to process this new information. I'm not a complete idiot, and I know that Leal could be fucking with me, but I don't think so. There'd been a confidence in his voice, a cockiness that told me everything I needed to know.

Charlie hadn't set me up. She hadn't sealed my parent's fates. My brothers had been wrong.

I'd been wrong.

CHAPTER ELEVEN

I missed you too.

Charlie

I'm bathed in darkness, but my mind must be playing tricks on me. My head is hung forward, and I'm staring down at where I'm certain my wrist must be. I shouldn't be able to see it. I can't see my hand, or the white zip tie, or the chair, so there's no way I can be seeing the figure eight tattoo on my wrist. Logically, I know this, but right now I'm watching it glow.

I wonder if this is my mind playing a cruel joke on me, making that tattoo the only thing visible.

Light brightens the room, and I jump in the chair and slam my eyes shut. The throbbing in my head turns into a sharp pang, but I force my eyes to crack open so I can make out the little figure eight on my wrist. It's still black.

Metal clangs and the door to the room opens, but I don't look up. I'm too fucking tired to play any more games.

Footsteps sound on the concrete until a set of boots enter my vision. I know who it is by the way the oxygen seems to leave the room and the way my spine sizzles with his eyes on me, but I still don't look up.

I turn my head when a knife enters my line of sight, and the zip ties are cut, freeing me from the chair.

"Does the torture you have planned next not require me to be tied to a chair?" I bite out, not moving. There's venom in my voice, but there's also an ache that I hope he can't hear.

Calloused hands cup my jaw and force me to look up into the stormy gray eyes that have haunted my dreams for years. I don't see the anger I expect. I see regret. A lifetime of it.

He says nothing for what feels like too long. He just stares at me, either trying to memorize the lines of my face or he's lost in his own mind.

"What is it, Fender?"

He shakes his head and runs his thumb across my bottom lip, his eyes lowering there. "You didn't do it, did you, Charlie?"

I narrow my eyes. "No, I didn't. That's what I've been telling you this whole time. I—"

His thumb pressing over my lips quiets me. He weaves a hand around the back of my neck and pulls me forward an inch.

"I should've never let you go."

His thumb lifts from my mouth, and he replaces it with a brutal kiss. I struggle for a minute, lifting my hands to his chest and pushing against rock. When that doesn't work, I sink my teeth into his lip hard enough that the taste of his blood mixes with my own.

He yanks away for a second, running a finger over his bottom lip then holding it up to see the blood. When he looks down at me again, he only looks more hungry.

"I don't want you," I lie when he grabs my hips and yanks me to my feet. Tears have welled in my eyes, and I fight the urge to sniffle with my runny nose. "You never meant anything to me."

He lifts me, and I wrap my ankles around him on reflex. My nails dig into his shoulders. He backs us into a wall and starts kissing my neck, probably thinking better of moving to my lips again.

"I wish I would've let you die."

"Stop lying," he growls. He holds me up with one hand while he uses the other to yank my T-shirt over my collar bone. He nips at my flesh there, and I let my head lay back against the concrete.

I want to fight it, I really do. I feel like the moment I decided to come back to Oregon, I've been setting myself up to get hurt. By Fender, by my family, by everyone. I'm sick of it. I'm sick of caring what anyone thinks, and I'm sick of holding on to things that aren't there anymore. Just when I want to let go, Fender's holding on for me.

"Stop," I say, even as I'm craning my neck to grant him better access. He gropes my breasts and groans as he shoves my T-shirt up and pulls me forward so he can rip it over my head.

He sets my back against the wall again and buries his face in my cleavage, my tits pressed together by my black, lacy bra.

"Fender…"

He stills, and he lowers me some so we're face to face. His breathing is heavy, and he searches my eyes for something. The tears I haven't yet let fall make him appear blurry.

He closes his eyes and kisses me, softer this time. More like an apology than a demand.

I close my eyes as well and the first few tears slide down my cheeks. I wrap my hands around his neck and kiss him back, giving my own unspoken apologies.

I'm sorry I left.

I'm sorry it happened.

I'm sorry I'm one of them.

My back lifts off the wall, and Fender carries me, but I

don't open my eyes to see where we're going. He shifts my weight to free a hand for the door, but his lips never leave mine. I hope he never stops kissing me again.

He carries me up a flight of stairs and then white noise and voices fill the air. We walk through another door and are outside. I finally open my eyes when we take the first few steps away from the large building we were just in. Probably the clubhouse.

"Where are we going?" I ask, out of breath.

He shifts me again and pecks me a few more times. "Home."

My eyes widen, and I stiffen in his hold because I think he's talking about taking me back to the Black Savages, but he walks us up to a cabin back behind some trees. Home. *His* home.

I lean into his neck and smile against him so he won't see it. I was scared he'd take me back to my family, to safety. I'm fucking crazy.

I kiss his neck then work my way back to his lips. He pauses kissing me to open the front door, but I don't let him break away. It isn't until we're inside and he's prying me off him that I stop and let him toss me onto the bed.

I bounce only once before he's on top of me, his mouth latching onto my neck and his hands travelling up my sides.

He slips his hand under my bra and takes one of my puckered nipples between his thumb and finger. I bite my lip and throw my head back with a groan when he pinches down hard.

"Do you have any idea how long I've waited for this?" Fender asks, winding a hand around my back to unhook my bra.

I peer at him through half-hooded lids and wiggle to help him pull my jeans off. I'm left in only my panties.

"You're *mine*, Charlie. I'm not letting you leave again. Ever. Do you understand me?"

"Fender…"

"*No.*" I'm taken aback by the intensity in his tone, the ferocity of it. He sounds angry, and I think maybe I imagined the tenderness coming from him only minutes ago. "You might not have done what we took you for, but you're still a prisoner. You're *my* prisoner. You aren't leaving again."

"Are you trying to convince me or yourself?"

"Shut up." He fists my hair and yanks me to his lips. The kiss comes so hard and so fast, I don't have time to respond to it before he shoves me back and flips me over.

The sound of my panties ripping fills the room, and a thick finger plunges into me a moment later. I suck in a sharp breath and curl my nails into the edge of the mattress. It's been months since anyone has been inside me, and four years since a man has been able to make me come. Fuck, I need this.

Fender pumps a digit into me, and it feels like the friction he's making ignites a fire that travels to my clit. I push my ass back, hitting his palm, and he chuckles before adding another digit and sliding his other hand around my front and finding my clit. "Is this what you want?"

I moan as he strokes my bundle of nerves with an expert touch, and my shoulders shake with a shiver.

Every thrust of his fingers sends me closer and closer to the edge until I'm dangling off a cliff. I want to fall, but Fender's holding onto my fingertips. I push my hips back, but he lets up the pressure and holds me at the point just before I explode.

"Fender!"

"What do you say?" he taunts, heat and amusement in his tone.

I bite my lip and push my hand down my front, but he's blocking me from my clit. My body is wound so tight with tension, I swear I might break.

"Beg for it."

"Please!"

"Please what?"

"Please, Fender, make me come."

He pulls his fingers from me and runs his hand over my back before shoving my face into the pillow. His lips press to my lower back. "Good girl."

I gasp when he lifts my hips and splays me open. Cool air touches my slick folds, but it only lasts a second before Fender's warm tongue slides into me.

My mouth drops open in a moan, and my grip on the mattress tightens while his tongue fucks me and he rubs his thumb on my clit.

I clench my eyes shut and scream into the pillow when my muscles ripple and I come on Fender's face. He doesn't stop then. He starts lapping at me like a hungry dog, and I'm building up to another orgasm when he finally pulls away. He drops me to my knees, and I look back to see him violently ripping off his clothes.

He climbs behind me and weaves a hand through my hair. He yanks my head back as he slams into me, and I cry out as my eyes burn. It's been way too fucking long.

"Tell me you're mine," he grunts as he ruts into me.

He's fucking me so hard it feels like he's splitting me open, so I can't do what he's asking even if I wanted to. My mouth hangs open, and I'm frozen like this.

He pulls harder on my hair, and my neck bends to the point of pain. "Tell me you're mine, Charlie."

He fucks me harder like his frustration is fueling him, and I suck in a deep breath and try to think through the fog.

"You first," I manage to get out.

He slows a moment, nearly pausing, but then he lets go of my hair and picks up his pace. My face falls against the pillow, and I suck in sharp breaths. I sway my hips to meet each of his thrusts, and when my second orgasm comes, I clench my jaw so hard I think my teeth might shatter.

Fender's close. I can tell by the desperation in his grunts and thrusts. It's crazy how familiar this feels. How many things I can remember now that we're here. Like the scent of our sex and the feel of sweat dripping onto my back. The way his pillow smells of him, and how it feels to inhale deeply with my face in it.

Fender slides a hand up my stomach and cups one of my tits. He pumps into me with several merciless thrusts before he pauses and grunts as he fills me.

His heavy, warm breath skates over my shoulders, and his fingers digging into me relax. He pulls out and collapses beside me, pulling me into him as he does.

I roll over to face him and stare into his half-hooded eyes.

"I missed you," he whispers, smoothing my hair back and then tugging me closer possessively.

I give a small smile and kiss his lips. When I pull back, his eyes are closed, and he doesn't open them. I let my gaze drift over the vein protruding from his neck, down his collarbone, and to his pec where the infinity tattoo rests next to his club's symbol. My heart drops into my stomach, and I reflexively touch my wrist. I thought he would have covered that up by now.

I press my ear to the tattoo on his chest and listen to his heart beating out of control.

"I missed you too."

CHAPTER TWELVE

With her here, so close, I feel lighter than I have in years, and inexplicably heavier.

Fender

"So, now what?"

I peel my eyes open and come face to face with a pair of green irises staring back at me. Charlie's dark hair frames her face, and with her head above me like it is, it teases my chest. It took hours for my heartbeat to slow last night, but it has yet to return to normal.

"I dunno." I shrug, knowing I need to give her a better answer than that but not sure if she's on the same page.

Charlie's eyes narrow, and her body tenses, even as she pulls her bottom lip between her teeth in a gesture that I recognize as insecurity and frustration. Sure, we've fucked, but we've both learned the hard way that sex isn't going to hold two people together. Especially when those two people were raised to hate each other.

I cup her cheek with my hand, and her palm covers it, seemingly to hold it in place. The infinity symbol tattoo on her wrist taunts me, reminds me that there was a time when nothing else mattered. Not our clubs' rivalry, not a complicated past. There was no death between us, not to mention betrayal, heartache, and anger. Four years ago, things were simpler... sort of.

"Forget it," Charlie grumbles as she shoves my hand away from her face and pushes herself away from me.

I snatch her arm and roughly pull her back while sitting up to fuse my lips with hers. It takes a few agonizing moments for her to react, to return the kiss at all, but when she does, it feels like home. I thrust my fingers into her hair and hold her face steady while our tongues tangle.

"Some things never change," she mumbles when we break the kiss.

"What's that supposed to mean?"

"Nothing."

Charlie extricates herself from my arms and scoots to the side of the bed. She draws her knees up to her chest and wraps her arms around them, almost as if to shield herself from me. My stomach twists at the action, a mixture of frustration and fury. I sit up and swing my legs over the edge of the bed, my back to her.

"Why do you have to be so goddamn difficult?"

I stand and a smug grin tugs the corner of my lips up when her sharp intake of breath reaches my ears. I'm naked and I know she's seeing all the new ink I've gotten over the last few years. I can't help but wonder if she's noticed the one that has her name hidden in it.

"I, uh... wow," she says on an exhaled breath.

I pick up my discarded jeans from last night and tug them up my legs, leaving them open at the waist. I turn around to face her, and the heat in her expression makes me grateful I did because my dick hardens and seems to point at her like a heat seeking missile.

I cross my arms over my chest, enjoying the flush of her skin as her eyes travel over my body like a physical caress.

"Keep that up and we're not gonna make it out of this fucking room today."

Charlie shifts to her knees and crawls across the bed until she reaches the edge. Her arms stretch out, and she wraps her hands around my biceps to pull me closer. I can't help but let her. I've missed her, and while I no longer know how to be the guy she once knew, I do know how to let sex do my talking.

A growl escapes me, and she moves her hands to my chest to stop my advance. When I do, she lets her arms fall to her sides and plops down on her ass. Confusion swirls around me. One minute, she's doing everything to invite me in, and the next she's putting up barriers. It's fucking infuriating.

"Fender, can we talk?"

"About what?" I ask, suspicion dripping from my tone.

"I don't know." She shrugs. "Anything… everything."

"That doesn't exactly narrow it down."

"No, I guess it doesn't. It's just…"

"What, Charlie? Just fucking spit it out."

She takes a deep breath and turns her head to stare at the wall. When she releases the breath, she returns her attention to me.

"Don't get me wrong, I'm happy to be out of that… well, whatever that room was, but why am I?" She pins me with her stare, and I feel exposed in a way I hadn't when we were fucking. "It's like a flip switched. One minute you hate me and the next you're jumping my bones."

I drop my chin to my chest and let out a sigh. I don't exactly know how to explain it to her. All I know is I've spent years hating her, wishing I'd never let her in my life, and it took an hour, an *actual* set up by the Black Savages to make me realize that maybe I'd been wrong. Rather than go into all of that, I decide to fall back on an age-old explanation used by MC's all over the place.

"You know I can't discuss club business."

"Oh, bullshit," she exclaims as she shoots off the bed and gets to her feet.

I turn away from her and walk to my dresser. "Don't. Don't do that. You of all people know how it is." I rummage through my clothes until I find what I'm looking for. "Here," I toss a black cotton tee at her. "Put this on."

She holds the tee in front of her and scowls before huffing out a breath and pulling it over her head. The garment hangs down to mid-thigh, and my chest squeezes at the sight of her with the Infinite Motor's logo across her tits. Even when I'd done everything I could to bury the memory of her, I hadn't been able to completely let go. Our matching tattoos would forever be a part of us, and I had to go and link the symbol to my fucking business.

"Put your jeans on," I demand. "I wanna take you somewhere."

I don't wait for her to do as she's told. I make my way to the adjoining bathroom and take a leak. When I return to the bedroom, Charlie's standing there, fully dressed. The Infinite Motors tee is pulled to the side at her waist and tied in a knot, exposing a hint of tanned flesh just above the waistband of her skintight jeans. Instantly, I'm hard, harder than I was earlier.

"Where are we going?" she asks as I grab her hand and tug her out of the house and down the steps.

There's laughter in her voice and I realize, in that moment, that I'd do anything to be able to hear that laugh every day for the rest of my life, especially knowing I put it there.

"You'll see."

When we reach the garage and I throw the door open, Charlie digs in her heels. I glance at her, unsure of how to read her expression. Her eyes are wide, and her hand is covering her mouth. She's either shocked or pissed, neither of which I'm completely comfortable with.

"What? You really thought I'd leave it in the fucking mall parking lot?" I ask, hoping it's shock she's feeling. At least that won't necessarily result in a fight.

"I, uh, I don't know what I expected." She takes the last few steps toward her bike and lifts a leg to straddle it. Her lips tilt into a smile, and she beams at me from the leather seat.

"Okay." I draw the word out. "At least you're smiling."

I straddle my own bike and start the engine. Charlie does the same and we both rev 'em up, letting the roar echo off the walls. There's nothing better than a metal beast you know you have the power to control. Pussy maybe, depending on the chick. Charlie's pussy? Definitely better.

"Follow me. It's not too far."

I pull out of the garage, and she's close behind me. I lead her off of Soulless Kings' property and toward the Coastal Highway. We used to ride up and down the coast for hours. When was the last time she did this? Did she ride where she'd been? Shit, where *had* she been?

Thirty minutes later, we reach the spot, the place I want her to see. I haven't even brought any of my brothers here, and for a moment, I feel like I'm being disloyal to them. Charlie may not have set us up all those years ago, but she's still the Black Savages' princess and sharing *anything* with her that I don't share with them seems wrong somehow.

We park our bikes and stretch our legs. I walk to the edge of the cliff and look out at the ocean below, not for the first time feeling like I'm somehow insignificant in this big world.

"This is incredible."

Charlie stands next to me and takes in the same scenery. With her here, so close, I feel lighter than I have in years, and inexplicably heavier. We have a lot to talk about, to catch up on, which is why I brought her here, to the place I go when I have a lot on my mind.

I need Charlie, more than I've ever needed anyone, but I

also recognize that we don't know each other anymore. Not the people we are now. Suddenly, my palms are sweating and every nerve ending buzzes with apprehension.

My next move is either going to be the smartest thing I'll ever do or the one thing in my life that I'll always regret. I turn to face Charlie and stare at her until she faces me. I force a smile, even though it feels stupid. *I* feel stupid.

Questions dance in her eyes, and she tilts her head when I don't speak. After a few deep breaths and a fucking mental pep-talk, I push the words past my lips.

"Hey. I'm Chris, but the ladies call me Fender."

CHAPTER THIRTEEN

For all of the changes he's made, for all of the years he's grown older, I still feel the same.

Charlie

Fender's crooked smile draws my eyes, and they drift to the slight discoloration on his canine. Half of it is fake, and I remember it catching my eye the first night I met him, as well. The first time he said that exact line to me.

I cover a hand over my mouth and snort. I try to suppress a laugh, but I don't last long before I'm clutching my stomach, which is now aching from my laughter.

His lips tic and after a moment, he laughs with me. "What, too cheesy?"

"No." I shake my head and wipe moisture from under my eye. "No, it's exactly something you would do."

I mean that... I think. He looks just like the old Fender right now with his sexy, but almost boyishly cute half-grin and his gray eyes that don't look quite so hard. He looks so much like him that I can forget for a moment that that version is gone. I guess I don't really know him anymore, and maybe that's his point.

I hold out my hand. "I'm Charlotte. The guys call me Charlotte."

He takes my hand and shakes. "Charlotte," he coos, almost exactly as he did the night we met. "No offense, but you don't look like a Charlotte."

"Oh?"

He shakes his head. "Nah, more like a Charlie. I think I'll call you that."

"How do you know you'll get the chance? You might not ever see me again."

He smiles, and unlike that night, it's a little sad. "I'll take my chances."

The words are exactly the same as they were when we first met, but everything else is different. Not better or worse, just... different.

Slowly, my smile falls and I rest my hand in my lap. Water splashes against rock beneath us, and I move my gaze to watch. It's beautiful out here. Chaotic with the waves crashing and then calm when the water eases back out into the ocean.

"Where did you go for all those years, Charlie? What happened to you?"

What happened to me? Nothing. I spent four years chasing things that weren't there and wondering what if. For all of the changes he's made, for all of the years he's grown older, I still feel the same. I want to tell him this, but I answer his first question instead.

"South Carolina." I glance at him and notice the incredulous look in his eyes. "What?"

"You needed that much distance between us?"

"I needed that much distance between me and this town. Believe it or not, Fender, it wasn't all about you."

"Then what was it all about?"

I look away again and feel my shoulders bunch as I pretend to peer out at the ocean unaffected. My heart speeds up at the memories assailing me. I can smell the blood from that night, but it's only coming from one person in my mind. The man I shot. My *family*.

When I say nothing in response to his question, he fills the silence.

"Oh... right." Fender shifts closer to me and wraps his arm around my back. "I don't know why I keep forgetting how you saved me."

"Because you don't want to believe I saved you."

"Yes, I do."

I don't respond and Fender sighs into me before wiping a palm on his jeans. "I had just seen my family murdered, it was the most horrific night of my life. I know I did you wrong, Charlie. I know that, and I'm so fucking sorry. But what was I supposed to do? I wasn't in the right frame of—"

"You could've listened to me."

"You were one of them."

His words burn, and I try to pull away from him, but his arm at my waist holds me in place. I turn to him with a glare. "I *am* one of them."

I expect him to glare back and for his comforting touch to turn rough, but it doesn't. He frowns at me, his gaze moving between my lips and my eyes. "Maybe I don't want you to be."

My glare falls and I turn my head to face the water again. I lace my fingers on my lap and tap my thumbs.

He's said that to me once before, and I know exactly what he means by it. Leave the Black Savages. Come be with him as a Soulless Kings' whore or some shit like that. As if that's a possibility. As if I'd ever even want that.

"MC princess to club whore. That's quite the downgrade."

"You wouldn't be a club whore. You'd be mine."

"Ah, only *your* whore? Now I feel special."

I go to stand, but Fender presses on my thigh to keep me

in place. I turn to face him, and the relaxed Fender is gone. This is the new version. The hardened version.

"That isn't what I meant."

"Do you want to know what I've been doing this whole time?"

He lifts his hand from my thigh, and I pull my legs up and shift to face him. I don't wait for him to answer before I continue.

"I've been a waitress, a bartender, a hotel maid, and a receptionist for a mechanic. The last job I got because I wanted a reminder of you. I've lived in three different towns in South Carolina and have had three different shitty one bedroom apartments. I worked, I ate, I slept. That was my life. Every single day I spent trying to get over you and trying to get over what I did for you, and I never succeeded. You may have transformed into this new person, but I'm the *same* girl, Fender. The same one who told you no back then. My mind hasn't changed, and it will never change."

Fender doesn't try to stop me when I stand this time. I stomp back over to my bike, my hands shaking at my sides. I ball them into fists to make it not as noticeable and wait for Fender to catch up.

Then it hits me. Why am I waiting for him? I'm his prisoner, not his guest. Fuck him. I climb on my bike, but before I can start her up, Fender grips my wrist. I snap my head to look at him.

"Careful, Charlie."

"Careful of what?"

He takes the key from the ignition and slips it into his pocket, his serious eyes never leaving me.

"The Soulless Kings don't feel the same way I do about you. No decision has been made saying you can go home."

"Aren't you the president?" I sneer.

He gives a single nod. "I am, but I'm not a dictator, and I'm not the only person affected by your club's savage ways."

"So what then? You're going to take me back to torture me some more? Maybe pass me around like I'm some sort of trophy?"

"No." Fender's expression softens, and he brushes my wind-blown hair off my shoulders before meeting my eyes again. "I'm going to take you back and show them the girl I fell in love with. As soon as they know who you are, they won't vote to do anything to you… Then you'll be free to go."

I study him closely, trying to gauge if he really means it. Yesterday, he was telling me I was never leaving. That I was his.

As much as I want for that statement to be true, I can't have it. My father died a Soulless Kings' rival, and it'd be disrespectful to his memory for me to become one of them. Even if I didn't care about loyalty to my family, I wouldn't be Fender's because he would never be mine. Not this version of him.

As I stare into his eyes, I can't help but want the opportunity to know this version. I wonder if I could love him too.

"I'll be free to go. Just like that?"

He gives a sad smile and nods. "Just like that."

CHAPTER FOURTEEN

I want to give her the life of a queen so she'll leave her life as a princess behind.

Fender

"What the fuck, man?"

Joker is leaning against the bar, a half-empty beer bottle in his hand. Margo is behind him wiping up some invisible mess in hopes of overhearing information she shouldn't. She knows that I know what she's doing, but I'm too tired to give a shit.

"You got something you need to get off your chest?"

"As a matter of fact…"

Joker shifts his glare from me to the others in the room. His face is hard, determined, but his scowl only deepens when he realizes he's alone in his challenge of me. AC/DC is pumping through the speakers, brothers are being blown by Bangin' Betties and the drugs and alcohol are freely flowing. I'd hoped the party would conceal my actions, but of course Joker would be the one to actually be paying attention.

"I can't hear you." I'm taunting him, practically daring him to push me further. I know what he wants to say and while it pisses me the fuck off, he's not wrong.

"Why is that bitch in your room and not the basement?"

Tension coils my muscles, and my jaw tics. I glance at Margo and raise a finger, indicating for her to get me a drink. She turns to do my silent bidding and returns with a beer and a shot of tequila. I down the shot and slam the glass on the bar top before chugging half of the beer. When I'm satisfied that I can keep my cool, I return my attention to Joker. He's staring at me, incredulous. He's crossed a line and he knows it, but he's not scared. He's never scared.

"You have no fucking clue what you're talking about." The words come out gritty.

"Oh no?" Joker pushes off the bar and steps toward me. "Please, set me straight."

Before I know what's happening, my hand is around his throat and I've got him bent back over the bar top, my face inches from his.

"This is the one and only warning you're gonna get, brother. Where I keep my woman is none of your goddamn business. Got it?"

"What's going on?"

Piston's voice registers behind me a second before his hand lands on my shoulder. I increase the pressure of my fingers around Joker's neck for a brief moment, and then I let go and take a step back. Joker stands and adjusts his cut, his face red. It's not clear if it's from rage or embarrassment at having been caught being put in his place.

"Nothin'," I respond to Piston.

I down the rest of my beer and tip the empty bottle to Margo. She grabs me a fresh one and hands it to me.

"Didn't look like nothin' to me." Piston rocks back on his heels, his hands in his pockets.

"Did you know what he was…"

Joker's words trail off as I storm away, toward the stereo. I stab a finger at the power button and kill the music, silence blanketing the room. There's a chorus of groans, and all eyes turn to me.

"I'm gonna say this one time and one time only, so fucking listen." I take another sip of my beer, the bitter brew settling in my stomach like battery acid. "I'm the president of this club, and I will do whatever I want, whenever I want, however I want." I walk to the center of the room and spin in a circle with my arms stretched wide. "You got a problem with that, you bring it to me. But for fucks sake, show some respect when you do."

Hushed murmurs break out, but no one speaks loud enough for me to make out the words.

"Jesus fucking Christ! If you've got something to say, have the balls to say it loud enough for me to hear."

Joker takes a few steps toward me and crosses his arms over his chest. He's a big motherfucker, and in that moment, all I can think is 'the bigger they are, the harder they fall'.

"Since when do we keep the enemy anywhere other than the Nightmare Room?"

"I'm not the enemy."

I whirl around at the sound of Charlie's voice. She's standing in the doorway between the main room and the hallway, and she looks like an avenging angel. I glance around the room and notice I'm not the only one staring at the biker beauty. When my eyes land on Joker, it's easy to see how tense he is. He seems frozen in place, but I know better.

Joker advances on Charlie, and I want to block him, protect her, but I am also keenly aware of the fact that nobody else believes she's innocent in all of this. Well, no one but Piston and even his belief is tenuous at best.

Apparently Piston has more faith in her than I think because he *does* step in front of Joker and puts his hand on his chest.

"You don't want to do that," he warns.

"The hell I don't," Joker shouts. He's straining against

Piston, and it takes everything in me to let this play out. "She's the fucking bitch that destroyed our club."

"Jesus, Joker, look around." Piston's free hand sweeps out to indicate the room. "Do we look destroyed to you?" I can't see Joker's reaction, but Piston relaxes a bit. "We've got Fender to thank for that, so I suggest you watch it before you say or do something you can't come back from."

"I, um…" Charlie walks around the two men and comes closer to me. The look on her face is a mixture of resignation and defiance. "Can I say something?"

"There's nothing—"

"Let her speak," I demand, cutting Joker off.

Charlie gives me a smile, but it's tentative, wary. She makes a point of looking around the room and making eye contact with every brother present. Hell, she even seems to connect with the Bangin' Betties. If she's scared, she's not showing it. She's smarter than that. She knows that if she shows some respect, she'll earn some in return.

"I know everyone thinks I had something to do with what happened four years ago." She pauses and takes a deep breath, squaring her shoulders in the process. "I can even see why you would think that, but I swear to you, I had nothing to do with it."

"Why should we believe you?" Riker's voice booms across the room.

"Because I'm telling you the truth."

"Which is exactly what you would say if you were lying."

Riker moves to stand next to me. His sheer size intimidates most *men*, but not Charlie. She's a force to be reckoned with, like all of my brothers. They just don't know it. Yet.

"Don't believe me." Charlie shrugs as if it's no skin off her back. "I don't fucking care. What I do care about is Fender. I won't stand by and watch him be disrespected because of something I didn't do."

Well, shit. She's standing up for me. While I can appreciate the gesture, I don't need her making me look like a fucking pussy that needs his battles fought by a pint-sized pixie. Granted, she's a badass pixie, but still.

In an effort to maintain some sort of control over the situation, I grab Charlie by the arm and drag her to my bedroom. Once there, I slam the door shut behind us.

"What the fuck was that?" I demand.

Her eyes grow round, but it isn't more than a second before they narrow and she advances on me, shoving a pointed finger into my chest.

"*That* was me saving your ass… again."

"I don't need you to fight my fucking battles, princess."

Charlie flinches, backing up a step as if I slapped her. The progress we made earlier seems like a lifetime ago. I meant every word I said to her. She's mine and I want everyone to know she's mine. But part of being mine means letting me handle anything club related.

"Try to get some sleep." I nod toward the bed. "I'll be back later."

Without waiting for a response, I turn on my heel and walk out of the room, pulling the door shut behind me. Back in the main room, the shouting is deafening. I bang my fist against the wall to get everyone's attention. All eyes turn to me, and I let the silence hang in the air for a moment before speaking.

"All voting members, church, now." I point in the direction of the office. "Everyone else, get the fuck out."

I don't wait to see if anyone does as they're told. I make my way to the office, deposit my gun in the designated box and move to the head of the long oval table. With my arms crossed over my chest and legs braced apart, I stare straight ahead and wait.

Piston is the first to enter the room, with Joker, Riker, and Greaser right behind him. They put their weapons with mine. When Joker steps up to the table, I glare at him. He stares back, but after a minute, he retraces his steps and pulls the knife out of his boot and adds it to the box. Once everyone is present, Piston calls church to order.

"Riker, I need you to fill everyone in on what happened when we went to take care of business with Bull."

Riker stands and explains about the Black Savages being the supplier Bull was screwing us with. He goes into explicit detail about every fucking second of the job, leaving nothing out and nothing to the imagination.

"Any questions?" I ask when he's done. When there are none, I continue. "Good. Now," I turn to look at Piston. "Care to explain what we learned from Leal?"

Piston stands and looks around the table. When his gaze lands on Joker, he maintains eye contact and speaks as if he's speaking directly to him.

"We now know that Leal is the new president of the Black Savages. He also said some things that led us to believe that Charlotte had no clue what was going to happen."

Joker stands so fast his chair crashes to the floor behind him. "And you fucking believe him? Even if Leal is telling the truth, that bitch is Dyno's—"

"That's the last time that word leaves your mouth when you're talking about Charlie," I growl. "We were wrong about her, end of story."

"And you came to this conclusion all on your own?" Burly asks quietly. He's not the type to question me, but as the club chaplain, he doesn't shy away from the tough questions.

"He and I talked about it, and we're in agreement." Piston answers before I even have a chance to open my mouth. "Charlotte had nothing to do with what happened."

"That still doesn't change the fact that she's one of them," Joker insists.

"You're right. It doesn't." I take a deep breath and hold it for a moment before continuing. "But as your president, as your *brother*, I'm asking you to trust me. Not Leal. Not Charlie. *Me*."

"I don't see how you're giving us much of a choice."

Joker turns to pick up his chair and sits down with a thud. He's pouting like a little bitch baby, and I'm getting close to my limit with his shit.

"You always have a choice. I'm not holding you here. You don't agree, you want no part of this, of me?" I tilt my head toward the door. "Don't let it hit ya in the ass on your way out."

When Joker makes no move to stand, I know he's coming around. It's hard to let go of the years of hatred, of the singular idea that you knew who the enemy was. Trust me, I know. I let everyone else's thoughts, fears, anger, get to me and turn me against Charlie. I've changed since that night, and I'm not the same man I was. Hell, I barely recognize myself anymore.

But I do know this: I'm a Soulless King. Always have been and always will be. And more than anything, I want Charlie by my side. I want my family to accept her as one of us. I want to give her the life of a queen so she'll leave her life as a princess behind.

"I don't care if you don't like her, but you will show respect to Charlie. As long as she's with me, she's to be treated like an ol' lady. She's not one of the Bangin' Betties you can stick your dick in. She's not your bitch, not your toy, not your anything."

"We get it, prez," Riker grumbles.

"Good. Now that we've cleared that up, anything else?" They all shake their heads. "We'll have church again tomorrow night. For now, go home."

Piston bangs the gavel, and my brothers disperse. Joker hangs behind, and when everyone else is gone, he squares his shoulders.

"What the fuck could you possibly want now?" I'm tired

and all I want to do is go back to my room and crawl into bed with Charlie.

Assuming she's even in the bed. Maybe she's on the floor, just to spite you.

"I know I got out of line earlier, but I mean no harm." Joker's face falls and he no longer looks like the cocky motherfucker I know. I put him on the spot and told him he could leave. Apparently, that was enough to scare him straight. "Just lookin' out for you, Fender."

"I know." I sigh because I *do* know. Joker is loyal as shit and he wouldn't put up such a fight if he didn't really believe in his reasoning. "Look, I'm beat. What's done is done. Just don't let it happen again. Ya got me?" I arch a brow.

"I got ya."

"Great. See you tomorrow."

We clasp hands and slap each other on the back, in that manly way of bikers. Once Joker is gone, I retrieve my gun from the box and head toward my room. I have no idea what kind of welcome I'm going to get, but I feel lighter than I have in four years so I don't really care. Charlie can scream, lash out, call me every name in the book. That's fine. Because at the end of the day, she's here, in my room, and we're together.

For now.

CHAPTER FIFTEEN

What makes you think you're so much better than the Black Savages? What makes you think I don't want to be one of them?

Charlie

I lay awake staring at the ceiling. It's dark but it isn't anything like the room they kept me in before. There's a window to my left with a sheer curtain draped over it that lets some of the moonlight shine in, and it would allow me to make out Fender's face if I turned his way, but I don't.

The music coming from outside the room stopped hours ago, so I'm assuming everyone is asleep. Everyone except me.

We're staying at the clubhouse tonight, and I assume it's because no one trusts me not to run from Fender's cabin. I wouldn't, but I'm not sure if it's because of the security on the property or if I just don't *want* to. I can't seem to decide.

Fender stirs in his sleep and rolls onto his side, wrapping his arm around me. I consider scooting away from him, but I'm already on the edge of the bed. Despite having explosive sex again tonight, letting him hold me feels too intimate, too much like the past.

I lay there for another half hour or so before my full bladder catches my attention. Inching my way out from under Fender's arm, I swing my legs off the bed and slowly stand, careful not to make too much noise.

I tiptoe from the room and creek the door shut behind me, letting go of the knob when I hear the click. When I turn around, I'm met with darkness. I was right, everyone's asleep.

I make my way down the hall and shut the door to the bathroom before flipping on the light. The last thing I want right now is to wake someone up and run into them waiting outside the door, so I hurry and grit my teeth at the sound of the toilet flushing and the sink running.

I finish up and pad down the hall back to the room, but a light in the bar area catches my eye. I pause in the entryway to the main room and squint my eyes at the bar. There's a single bulb on above it, and it casts a shadow on a man drinking from a glass. Bodies litter the floor, and a couple is sprawled, naked, on the couch. Apparently not everybody has a room in this house.

The man turns towards me, and I suddenly remember that I don't want to be seen. It's too late so I don't move a muscle. I just stare back and wait to see if he'll say anything. He doesn't. He turns back to face the wall and downs more of the liquid in the glass. Liquid that appears all too tempting.

My feet head in that direction before I can even think about it, like they have a mind of their own. When I get closer I see that the man is Joker, and that bit of info has me slowing down but not stopping completely.

"Can't sleep?" I ask, sliding onto the bar stool beside him.

"I must not be the only one." His words are light, but there's ice in his tone. Fender's promise to me enters my mind, telling me I'll be free to go as soon as the others agree to let me. I have a feeling Joker won't be easy to convince.

I lean over the bar and snatch a glass. Joker slides the

bottle of scotch in front of me without me having to ask for it.

"Thanks."

He gives a tight nod and takes another sip of his drink. I pour my glass and follow suit, closing my eyes as the liquor burns on the way down.

"You really know how to get into that guy's head, don't you?"

I scoff and roll my eyes, slamming the glass to the bar.

"You disagree?"

I turn to Joker and narrow my eyes. "It seems you're the one who's good at getting into his head, otherwise I wouldn't be here right now, would I?"

"If I had it my way you wouldn't be sitting on a barstool, having a drink next to me. You'd be in the Nightmare Room."

I prepare to hurl a comeback his way, but the lack of disgust in his voice holds me up. He isn't looking at me like he hates me right now, he's looking at me like he's trying to figure me out. He's looking at me like he's fucking sad.

"I didn't do it, Joker."

He holds my stare for a long moment. Finally, he breaks it and turns back to the wall behind the bar before taking a long drink.

I put more liquor back as well and set the glass on the bar top before climbing off the stool and turning to go back to the room. Before I can take the first step, Joker wraps a large hand around my arm and I snap back to face him.

"Would you like to know what he told us all tonight about how we're supposed to treat you?"

My jaw ticks, but I otherwise don't respond.

"He told us we're supposed to treat you as if you're his ol' lady. As if you're one of us." He pauses a minute to let that sink in. "He's never claimed one of our girls as his own, yet now he's claiming you. He loves you. I don't know why he loves you, I don't know what the fuck kind of pussy you have to have for him to fall in love with the enemy, but make no mistake, Charlotte, you're not one of us. You're one of them. The second you prove that and that'll be the end of whatever this is."

"What makes you think you're so much better than the Black Savages? What makes you think I don't want to be one of them?"

Joker says nothing, and I take the opportunity to pull out of his hold and stomp toward the bedroom, not caring anymore if I wake anyone up.

I step into the room and shut the door behind me and instantly note that the heavy breathing that filled the room earlier has ceased.

"You get lost?"

I carefully walk to my side of the bed and sit on the edge, resting my head in my hands. Fender's weight shifts the mattress, and his arm wraps around my waist. He drags me toward him, and I hesitantly lift up my legs and crawl to lay down beside him.

Now that my eyes have adjusted to the dark, I roam my gaze over the hard lines of his face, and I trail my fingertips over the ones by his eyes.

Fender takes my hand and presses it firmly to his cheek before dragging it down his neck and over his chest. His heartbeat pounds beneath my palm, and I trace the outline of the figure eight on his pec.

"What took you so long to come back to bed?" he asks.

"I was talking to Joker."

He tenses beneath my touch.

"And what did you talk about?"

"He said you told everyone they're supposed to treat me like I'm your ol' lady."

I study him carefully to gauge his reaction. I consider telling him everything else Joker said but decide against it. It isn't like Fender doesn't know what Joker thinks, so I don't see the point.

He nods. "That's right. I already told you, Charlie, I'm not trying to make you my whore."

"You didn't tell me you were trying to make me your ol' lady." My lips lift into a smirk, and I speak teasingly, but inside I melt a little bit.

"Well I am now."

My smirk falls, and I stare into cloudy gray eyes.

Fender cups the back of my head and pulls me to him for a kiss. I close my eyes and relax into it, my lips softening against his.

I breathe deeply through my nose and can smell a trace of oil that never seems to leave him, no matter how much hot water scalds him or how much soap he scrubs on the oil stains on his palms. The scent is always there.

I slide my hand further down his chest, over his abs, and into the waistband of his boxer briefs. Fender's teeth nip my lip as my fingertips graze over his tip, and I shove my hand further down and grip his cock. I squeeze and moan as he throbs in my hand.

His mouth leaves me abruptly, and he yanks my shirt from over my head while I work to get my shorts off. When he shifts to climb on top of me, I press a hand to his chest to stop him. I push him back and shove his boxer briefs down before straddling him.

"Fuck yes," he hisses when I slam myself down onto his cock.

My walls scream from being sore and it doesn't help that I don't give myself time to adjust, but I bite my lip and bounce on top of Fender through the pain. I'm not sure I've ever admitted this, but the pain is part of what I like. Just a little to give the pleasure an edge.

Fender's hands squeeze my tits as I ride him, and I go until my core tightens and I'm breathing heavy.

"Tell me you're mine," I demand, just to see if he'll say it. Just to see if it's true. The walls I'm building so desperately to protect myself here are paper thin hearing him say he wants me to be his ol' lady, but they haven't collapsed yet.

I slow my pace to try and get him to answer, but my core burns and I have to stop myself from speeding up to chase my release. Fender chuckles and lifts suddenly, gripping my sides to flip our positions and throwing me to the bed. He climbs on top of me and lowers his mouth to my ear to growl, "You know that's not the way this works."

I want to be disappointed, but my lips tug at the corners, and I'm turned on even more knowing he's as stubborn as I am.

Fender fucks me hard, and it takes no time before I'm screaming into his shoulder blade and my walls are spasming.

He stills and pants into my ear after he comes, and I listen to the sound like it's a lullaby, letting it pull me close to sleep.

He rolls off of me and takes me in his arms, tugging my head to his chest.

"You're fucking mine, Charlie. Whether you want to admit it or not."

My eyes flutter open for a minute and I'm staring straight at the infinity tattoo. I sigh against his chest before closing my eyes and pressing my lips against the ink.

Maybe he's right.

CHAPTER SIXTEEN

I don't just need her to be mine, I need her to be ours.

Fender

"Your girl's a screamer."

"Fuck you," I joke, flipping Piston the bird.

Piston's chuckle seems to echo off the hallway walls as I make my way to the bathroom. I wanted to wake Charlie up, tempt her into the shower with me, but she looked so peaceful sleeping that I couldn't bring myself to do it.

As hot water cascades down my body, I can't help but think about the last four years. When my parents were killed, I was devastated, but in the back of my mind, I knew I had Charlie to help me through it. Then she left, and my soul left with her. Seems fitting, being a Soulless King, that I'd actually feel, well, soulless.

When I hadn't been able to track her down, anger replaced sadness and then morphed into betrayal and hatred. My brothers had planted the seeds, and I let them take root and grow. Charlie was a Black Savage and while there'd always been a part of me, deep down, that knew she wouldn't set me up, I'd questioned it. So much so that I started to believe it and then I let it fuel me in a way that made me the man I am now.

After I'm clean, I wrap the brown towel around my waist and head back to my bedroom. Charlie is still curled up on my bed, and my lungs seize at the sight. I didn't think I'd ever have this again, have *her* again, yet here she is.

She's still a Black Savage.

I shake off the thought and gently jiggle her shoulder to wake her up. Her eyes flutter open, and a sleepy smile tugs at her lips.

"Mmm, what time is it?"

"Time for your pretty ass to get out of my bed."

Charlie bolts upright and her eyes narrow.

"You're kicking me out? Even after what we—"

"What? No, I'm not fucking kicking you out."

"But you said—"

"All I said was you need to get out of bed."

I drop my towel and let it fall to the floor. Charlie's green eyes widen and her tongue darts out to lick her bottom lip. I force myself to turn away and shuffle through my dresser to find clothes to put on because if I don't, we're gonna end up fucking and then I'll have to explain to my brother's why I'm late for church.

When I'm fully dressed, I return my attention to Charlie. She's on her knees, on the edge of the bed. I stride toward her and grip the back of her head to pull her in for a kiss. Our tongues collide, and I let the instant calm wash over me, the calm that only she can induce.

Charlie's moans fill my mouth, and I swallow them down, almost as if to hold them inside because I know they're going to have to last me at least a few hours. I grip her shoulders and urge her away from me. Her eyes are hooded and her cheeks are flushed. She's so fucking beautiful that it's difficult to tear my gaze away.

"I've got church. Why don't you grab a shower and get yourself ready for the day?"

"I don't have any extra clothes, Fender. And if you think I'm wearing some other chick's shit, you're dumber than you look."

She looks away, toward the wall, and I shake my head at her. She may be here and I may have staked my claim, but we've got a long way to go for there to be complete trust. I grab her chin and force her to look at me.

"First of all, I'm offended that you'd think I'd treat you like some desperate Bangin' Betty." She tries to avert her eyes, so I bend my knees and lean in close. "Second, I may not have been celibate the last four years, but there hasn't been anyone that's stayed long enough to have clothes left behind. And third, your bags from your shopping trip are in the closet." I tilt my head in that direction and let go of her chin.

Charlie glances toward the closet before her head drops to her chest. Her shoulders rise with her deep breath, and when she returns her attention to me, she releases it and her shoulders sag.

"Oh. Okay."

She scrambles off the bed and retrieves her purchases, throwing them across the mattress as if to take inventory of what she has. A particular shirt catches my eye, and I snatch it up to look at it. It's a black tank top with a pair of white angel wings spread across the chest. In the center of the wings is an infinity symbol.

"Wear this," I say as I toss the shirt at her.

Charlie glances at the tank. Indecision is written all over her expression, and I imagine she's debating on whether to argue with me, based on principle, or wear the damn shirt. She can bristle all she wants, but she bought the shirt for a reason and that reasoning will win out.

"What exactly are we doing today?"

"Does it matter?" I arch a brow and cross my arms over my chest.

"I need to know what we're doing so I know what to wear."

"I told you, that shirt." I nod toward the fabric that's now twisted in her hands. "Jeans and boots will be fine. Unless you'd rather go naked. Gotta say, I wouldn't mind but I'm not really in the mood to kill anyone today, so I wouldn't suggest it."

Charlie snorts with laughter, and I can't help but smile at the sound. She always did have an incredible laugh. It's one of those that come from deep within. It's not delicate, but it's real. I like real.

We both stand there for a few more minutes, her trying to gain some control and me debating on cancelling church so I can stay with her. I can't do that though. Too much to discuss. We're down to less than twenty-four hours before we're supposed to deliver her to the Black Savages. I'm not inclined to do that, but that means we'll need to plan for the attack Leal promised would come if we don't.

"I should be done in an hour. Feel free to hang out with Margo if you're done before me."

I don't wait for a response before leaving Charlie to do her thing so I can do mine. Normally, I wouldn't want to get Charlie mixed up with anyone in the club, but Margo won't treat her bad. If anything, she'll mother her. Besides, if she's going to be mine, then my brothers need to get used to seeing her around. I don't just need her to be mine, I need her to be ours. I need her to be part of the Soulless Kings' family.

"Are you sure about this?"

Piston blocks my exit after adjourning church. Despite

the questioning stares from the others, I decided not to put Charlie's surrender to a vote. I know I can't stall it forever, but I'm not quite ready to give her up. Besides, the Soulless Kings don't give in to the demands of the enemy. That means we need to prepare for an ambush, but we can handle it. After the last Black Savages attack, we've increased our membership and honed our skills. We've also gone up against them several times since then, and the Soulless Kings always come out on top.

"You aren't? If they follow through with Leal's threat, we can take the fuckers blindfolded and you know it."

"That's not what I'm talking about." Piston thrusts his meaty hand through his hair. "Are you sure Charlotte's worth all of this? Worth risking all of our lives for?"

I give the question some thought before answering. Not because I don't know the answer but because the answer seems to be important to Piston. He's not asking because of the club. If that were the case, he'd have brought it up during church. He's asking as my friend, my brother.

"P, she's worth it. She's everything."

I move past him and he falls into step beside me as we make our way toward the main room. It's still fairly early, too early for the normal crowd, but all of the patched members, as well as some prospects, are milling around.

I spot Charlie on a bar stool, talking to Margo. I stiffen when I see Trainwreck standing next to Charlie, with his hand on her shoulder. They're laughing and white hot rage boils my blood. A ringing starts in my ears, and the rest of the room fades away. I stalk toward them and shake off Piston's grip when he tries to stop me.

"You've got two seconds to get your fucking hand off my woman," I growl from behind Trainwreck.

He drops his arm and spins around to face me. Margo's face sobers and Charlie turns on her stool with her jaw dropped and her eyes wide.

"Fender!" Charlie scolds. "What the he—"

"If you want to be a Soulless King, you better learn the rules and learn 'em quick."

My hands are shaking, my body heat surging. He's lucky Charlie is sitting right here because that is the only thing stopping me from leveling him and kicking his ass to the curb.

"I meant no disrespect. It won't happen again."

Rather than respond, I nod my head. Trainwreck walks away, and I turn my attention to Charlie. Piston is standing next to me and he's shaking his head. Charlie looks like she wants to take a bite out of my hide.

"What?" I snap.

"I get that you have an image to uphold but shit, Fender, I can take care of myself. He wasn't doing anything wrong."

"Oh yeah? So you're telling me that the Black Savages don't handle that shit the same way, if not worse? Prospect touches a claimed woman, and he just gets away with it?"

"Not at all," she fires back. "It absolutely would be handled the same way. The problem with your thinking is that there's one glaring difference."

"What's that?"

"I'm not a claimed woman. Not by a Black Savage or a Soulless King. Just because you've said the words, just because you declare me yours… that's not enough to make it true."

"The hell it's not." She's pushing my buttons like only she knows how to do, and I have to admit, she's not wrong. She's not a Bangin' Betty, and if I want her to really be mine, to really belong to me, she has to want it as much as I do. I'm sure as hell not going to admit that to her though, not right now.

"You better wrap your head around this, Fender. I'm not some silly girl that's gonna fall at your feet or give in to your demands. I was raised to think for myself, to stand up for myself." She glances past me, and I follow her gaze to see that we've gained an audience. "Anyway, you shouldn't want that. It takes a strong woman to be with a man like you, an MC president. If you want someone who will stand beside you, who will challenge you and support you, I'm your girl. Otherwise, you might as well let me go now because I'll never be a shrinking violet."

"Damn."

I look over my shoulder at the source of that exclamation. Joker is standing there with a reluctant grin on his face.

"You got something to add," I ask.

"Nah." He shakes his head. "Although, even I have to admit, she may be the enemy, but she's not wrong. That *is* the type of woman we need at the top with you."

Not exactly the level of support I want from my brothers but it's a big step in the right direction.

"I get it, brother," Piston says with acceptance in his tone.

"Get what?"

"Why you say she's everything."

CHAPTER SEVENTEEN

I'm not different. Not that I can recognize, at least. We're different, together. Our situation is different.

Charlie

"Eww." Widow's nose scrunches and she squints at the bowl of coleslaw in front of me.

I chuckle and mix the contents. "You'll like it, I promise."

"On hamburgers? I don't think so."

"That was my first reaction too, but trust me. This shit's good."

"Are you sure you didn't get too much sun back in South Carolina?"

I stick out my tongue and finish up. Margo is working on deviled eggs and Widow is making a macaroni salad. There's a *ton* of food in here, and I'm still not sure it'll be enough to feed the pack of hungry men hanging around outside, taking advantage of the nice day. I completely forgot what it was like to feed so many people, but it's nice to cook for more than just me. And it's nice to share some of my Carolina taste with everyone. My cheeks hurt, and it's only now that I realize how much I've been smiling.

"Well, I for one am excited to try some good ol' Carolina cookin'," Margo says, giving me a toothy grin.

I smile back at her then step beside her and help her with the eggs. "Thanks, I appreciate that."

It took about five seconds to realize just how much I liked Margo. She isn't exactly the sort of old lady portrayed in the story books, but she still manages to be one of the kindest women I've ever met. Tattoos cover her loose skin, and she wears her gray hair up in a bun. She looks like, at one point, she was quite the badass and someone you wouldn't want to mess with. I'm not so sure I'd ever test that theory to see if that's only true in the past tense, but she's been nothing but nice to me since the moment we met.

Widow is the same way. She's got black hair and a red streak that hangs off the side of her face, hence the road name. And if that isn't enough, there's a black widow tattooed on her neck. She's younger than Margo, closer to Fender's age, and I know she has to have one hell of a story. I wouldn't have pegged either of these women as friendly, but they are quickly becoming the best friends I have in this house.

We finish preparing everything and begin carrying the bowls and trays of food out onto the back patio where there's a massive wooden table for days like today. A few heads turn our way and several of the bikers head inside to help us with the rest. That's one thing that's noticeably different from Black Savages' property. Nobody would've so much as glanced in our direction at home, but today Margo actually had to kick Trainwreck out of the kitchen because it was 'crowded.' They're not just a family here, they're a team. I like that.

I can feel Fender's eyes on me, but I don't look his way. We haven't spoken since our little scuffle this morning, but I don't think we're fighting or angry, at least I'm not. I just want him to have time to let what I said settle.

I go to take a seat, but a large hand cups my shoulder, and I spin around.

"You're next to me." Fender nods toward the end of the table. I raise my brow, and he rolls his eyes playfully. "Please?"

"Since you said 'please'."

I fight a smile at the snickers coming from those in earshot and follow Fender to the end of the table. Margo sits next to me, Piston sits across, and Joker is beside him. They all turn to Fender who hasn't sat down yet. He waits until everyone else is seated and is giving him their attention.

Fender raises a beer. "Let's thank the lovely ladies for preparing this meal and thank whatever god is out there for giving us some nice weather. It's about fucking time."

"Here here!" someone cheers in a drunken slur.

Several of the guys turn to Margo, Widow and I and thank us.

"To family," Fender says, raising his beer higher. Everyone at the table lifts their bottles and glasses, including me, and echo, "To family." I put my beer to my lips, an Oregon brew I didn't realize how much I missed, and take a long drink. It feels weird toasting to a family that isn't mine, but it doesn't register until I set my bottle on the wooden tabletop. I shake off the feeling and turn to Fender. Conversation ignites around me as people fill their plates.

"You and Widow seem to be getting along," Fender says, pulling my gaze to him. I didn't realize he'd been watching me today.

"Yep. I like her."

He leaves it at that, but it seems like he wants to say more. His mouth opens, closes, and doesn't open again.

I grab a hamburger and open the bun to put coleslaw on top. There's two bowls and I can see Widow at the other end of the table hesitantly doing the same.

"What the fuck are you doing?" Joker asks, disgust and amusement lighting up his words.

"Carolina thing." I load my burger up with the stuff just to gross him out more and smash my bun on top. I bring it to my mouth and moan dramatically as I take a bite.

Joker makes a sound, and Piston laughs.

"Carolina thing, huh?" Fender asks.

I nod and wipe a piece of coleslaw off my bottom lip.

Fender takes a big spoon of coleslaw and dumps it on top of his burger. I swallow my food and smile. "You don't have to try it."

"I need to see what they've been feeding you out there all this time." He winks, and whatever tension we had between us earlier today melts away. He takes a bite of his burger and makes a face for a split second before his eyes light up and he nods. Piston and Joker watch him carefully.

"Not bad," he says after he swallows.

Piston gives his head a shake. "All right, fuck it." He smothers his burger and bites into it like he's not worried about what he's eating. He pauses mid chew, and I chuckle when his expression turns queasy.

"It's not for everyone," I say through a laugh. Everyone around watching laughs as well.

Piston swallows it down and takes a swig of his beer. When he pulls the bottle away, he takes in a breath. "It's not bad. Just… different."

"Sometimes different is good."

I have one hand draped over the arm of my chair, and Fender takes it and pulls it halfway to him. He laces his fingers with mine. "I agree."

The way he says it makes me think he's talking about more than just coleslaw on a burger, and I can't help but wonder why. I'm not different. Not that I can recognize, at least. We're different, together. Our *situation* is different. Is he saying that's good? Is it better than it used to be?

"Charlie, you gotta tell us more about the Carolina crowd. What other shit are they into?" Piston asks. I don't miss that he called me Charlie. He used to, a really long time ago when Fender introduced me that way.

"Same things as here. The beaches are warmer, but that's the biggest difference. People like their bikes down there. I actually worked for a mechanic for a while. Cars instead of bikes, so I know a little about them now, too."

"Oh really?" Fender asks.

I nod. "Yeah, I mean, I was just a receptionist but I hung out in the shop when it was slow."

His jaw clenches and his hand tightens around mine without him seeming to notice it. I smirk. "Yeah, Old Man Nickels is a good guy. It was hard to leave him."

"Old Man Nickels?"

"The mechanic I worked for. He's seventy-five."

The hard line of Fender's jaw softens, and he turns to Piston and starts up a conversation about something else. I just watch him. I don't remember Fender being so jealous, but I kind of like it. Not with Trainwreck, mostly because I'm insulted Fender would think I'd ever be interested in a kid. I'm not sure the guy can even grow a beard. But I like that Fender wants me to be his. It makes me feel... wanted. At least somewhere.

I let go of Fender's hand and eat, making conversation with Margo in between bites.

After everyone's finished eating and conversations start to lull, I get up and take my plate inside. I toss the Styrofoam into the trash can in the kitchen and place my fork in the sink. When I turn around, Fender's there, leaning against the entryway.

"That was really good."

"Thanks," I say, walking toward him. "I'm glad you liked it."

"I didn't know you could cook."

I stop in front of him, and he pushes off the frame and wraps his hand around my waist.

"That's because I didn't used to."

"Ah." He bends and brushes my hair off one shoulder before kissing behind my ear. "See? Change is good."

I lean my head back and close my eyes as he kisses my neck. I want to give in to this, but I'm too distracted by a question lingering in my head.

"Why are you all here right now?"

"Hmm?"

"Shouldn't you be at the shop or something?"

He pulls back and plants a kiss on my forehead before standing up straight. I crane my neck to look up at him.

"We closed the shop for a few days. No schedule to keep."

"Why?"

He shrugs. "Does it matter? You sick of me already?"

"I have four years of not seeing you to make up for. No, I'm not sick of you."

The teasing smile he has plastered on his face falls, and he leans down and kisses me. He dips his tongue into my mouth, and I smile against his lips when I taste coleslaw. Fuck, I'm happy. Conflicted. Confused. Lost. But so fucking happy, at least in this moment.

Fender pulls back and presses his forehead to mine.

"A few of the brothers are still gonna go to the shop in a bit and get some work done. Wanna come? Show off your new skills?"

"They won't mind?" I ask, nodding toward the door to indicate the rest of the Soulless Kings that remain on the patio.

He doesn't say anything, and I suspect the answer is no, but I'm not totally sure. Most of the guys have given me the cold shoulder today, but Piston has opened up and Joker seems like he's trying. Trainwreck doesn't have a problem with me being here, and neither do Widow and Margo. It's like the club is divided, and I'm not sure how many people I'm supposed to warm up before they'll let me go.

My eyebrows knit as the thought hits me. I forgot I'm supposed to be trying to make them like me. I haven't even thought of it today. I haven't felt the need to even put in the extra effort. Today has just been... normal.

"We can always use an extra hand," Fender finally settles on.

I kiss him on the lips and let myself melt into it for a minute, drowning out the world around us and the situation we've managed to get ourselves into.

"Yeah," I say when I pull away. "I'm in."

CHAPTER EIGHTEEN

How am I supposed to be happy when I know that, in less than twenty-four hours, that feeling will likely be ripped away from me... again?

Fender

"Here, throw this on."

Piston tosses a greasy T-shirt to Charlie. When she catches it, her nose wrinkles, but other than that, there's no indication that she's disgusted by the dirty fabric.

"Bathroom's over there." I nod toward the half-closed door on the other side of the shop.

Rather than go to the bathroom, she turns to face the wall and changes out of her tank and into the T-shirt. She ties the shirt into a knot at her side, leaving a hint of smooth skin exposed. When she turns back around, Piston and Joker are staring at her with shocked expressions.

"What?"

"Ah, nothin'." Joker forces his gaze away and pretends to focus on the bike he's restoring.

"Please tell me you didn't make a habit of changing in front of Old Man Nickels?"

"Of course not," she scoffs.

"Good. Can we not make it a habit in front of these fuckers?"

"Oh, right. Sorry."

Charlie looks around the room and takes in all of the bikes we're working on. Her eyes light up when she sees the Indian Chief that's in front of Joker. She takes a tentative step toward it and glances over her shoulder as if asking for permission. When I nod, her steps quicken, and I can't help the grin that forms.

"Wow," she says on an exhale. "This is incredible, Joker."

"Still a hunk of metal, but when I'm done with it, it will be." Joker sucks at taking compliments and he's even worse when it's from someone that he's not quite sure about.

Charlie squats down and takes in the wheels before turning her attention to the gas tank. She seems to take in every line, every detail of the bike and mentally compare it to the information in her brain.

"It's a 1946, right?"

Joker's head snaps up, and I don't have to see the expression on his face to know he's shocked… and impressed. He nods.

"The badges on the gas tank are missing. Do you have those?" she asks.

Joker looks over his shoulder at me, and I shrug my shoulders. The sooner he realizes that this is a chick who knows her shit, the sooner he can quit fighting what he *thinks* he knows about her.

"Um, no, not yet." He walks around so he's standing on the same side of the bike as her. "Haven't been able to find originals, and the customer was crystal fuckin' clear: only original parts."

"I might be able to help you with that." Charlie bites the inside of her cheek as if wondering how he'll take that bit of information.

Joker snorts and Charlie's body tenses up. She steps

around the bike and walks toward me. When she's a foot in front of me, she holds out her hand, palm up.

"What?"

"I need your phone." Exasperation fills her tone.

"Why?"

"C'mon, Fender. Gimme your damn phone."

We stare each other down for a minute before I reach into my pocket and grab my cell. I hold onto it for a moment too long, and she snatches it out of my grip. Charlie walks through the swinging door into the front of the shop. Everything in me wants to follow her, make sure she doesn't walk out the front door, but I don't. I can hear her voice, and as long as I can hear her, she hasn't left.

When she comes back, she's got a smug smile on her face and her eyes are full of fire. She sets the phone down on the workbench behind me and returns to the Indian Chief. Joker doesn't acknowledge her presence as he continues to work on the carburetor. Piston and I exchange looks, but we're both equally confused. Charlie crosses her arms over her chest and starts to tap her foot, her annoyance at being ignored on full display.

"Jesus, what?" Joker snaps.

"Both the left and right badges for the gas tank will be here within a week."

Joker stands to his full height, causing Charlie to have to tip her head back to look him in the eyes. He reaches past her to grab a rag off of his workstation and rubs the grease from his hands. When he's done, he tosses the cloth back to where it was and mimics her stance, minus the tapping foot, but remains silent.

"The shifter knob, saddlebags, headlight and front and rear fenders will be delivered too." With each item she lists, she ticks them off with a finger. When Joker remains quiet, she adds, "I believe the words you're looking for are 'thank you.'"

"Who'd you have to fuck to be able to pull this off?"

"Watch your goddamn—"

Charlie holds up her hand to cut off my warning. She always was the type of girl who wanted to fight her own battles, and I'm glad to see that hasn't changed. I back down but remain prepared to strike if Joker keeps up his shit.

"I didn't have to fuck anyone, asshole."

"What did you just call me?" Joker growls.

"Oh grow up. There are worse things than 'asshole' that I could've called you and you know it."

Piston takes a step toward the pair, but I reach out and grab his arm, stopping him. If anyone is going to step in, it's going to be me, but for now, Charlie wants to handle it on her own.

"The way I see it, Joker, you've got two choices," Charlie says matter-of-factly.

"And those would be?"

"Well, you can keep sulking because I managed to get something done that you couldn't or," she pauses and takes a deep breath, "you can say 'thank you' and be grateful that you'll now have a new way to obtain original parts that you might not otherwise find."

"What the fuck way would that be? I don't work with just anyone."

"That's the best part." Charlie's face lights up as she smiles. "*You* don't have to work with anybody. *I* do."

"Huh?"

"Let me break it down for you. Old Man Nickels is a collector. He's got everything and anything you could ever want when it comes to vintage motorcycles."

"You're telling me that your old boss is willing to work with a man that he's never met, that he's going to hand over whatever I need?"

"No, I'm telling you that he loves me and he's happy to help *me* out... once I apologized for bailing without telling him, but that's beside the point. He wouldn't give *you* shit." Charlie chuckles and shakes her head.

"I thought you said he works on cars, not bikes," I say, not quite putting the puzzle pieces together.

"He does, but bikes are his passion." Charlie shifts her position so she can see all three of us when she speaks. "That's how we bonded. Like I said, he let me help out at the shop but after work he would open up the storage unit he had at the back of the property and tell me stories about his youth and about each and every part he had tucked away."

"That still doesn't explain why he's *giving* you these parts. They're worth a small fortune," Piston questions.

"Old Man Nickels has no family left. Never married, never had kids. When we realized that we both had a love of bikes, I became like a surrogate daughter to him." Charlie's eyes grow distant, almost like she's in another place, another time. "Man, I thought I knew all there was to know about motorcycles. He proved me wrong and taught me so much." Her gaze clears and she shakes her head as if to dislodge the memories. "Anyway, he's not getting any younger and he wants to see his collection be put to use so, I asked and he said yes."

Joker stands still and silent for a few minutes, seeming to take in all of the information. At first he's tense, frustration rolling off of him in waves, but he soon relaxes. Whether he's simply resigned himself to the fact that Charlie did something he couldn't or whether he's truly accepting her, I have no idea. At this point, I'll take either because both are progress.

"Thanks," Joker mumbles.

"What was that?" Charlie taunts.

"Fuck, I said 'thanks', okay?" he snaps back.

"You're welcome, Joker."

Charlie blows out a breath and appears relieved. She's not stupid so she knew the entire time she was talking that that could have gone a completely different way. Charlie comes to me and wraps her arms around my waist when she reaches me, her cheek resting on my chest. Just as my arms go around her, she straightens and throws a look over her shoulder.

"Joker?" she calls.

"Huh?"

"The seafoam blue would look killer on that bike." She shrugs. "Just sayin'."

Joker shakes his head and just as he starts to turn back toward the bike, I see the corner of his mouth tug up in a grin.

"Fuck, I'm beat."

Piston stretches next to the Harley he's working on. I glance at the clock on the wall and realize we've been at the shop for five hours. It's late and no doubt there's a party going on at the clubhouse without us. I know Joker and Piston probably wanna get back so they can find some pussy, and I'm sure as hell ready to get Charlie back to my room.

"Let's wrap it up and head back. We can pick up where we leave off tomorrow."

We all start to clean up our stations. Charlie helps me with mine, although she's spending more time distracting me by running her fingertips up and down my torso. The shop's AC doesn't always work, so I stripped down to my jeans earlier, as did Joker and Piston. Too bad they were there or I'd have stripped Charlie down too.

"Can I come back tomorrow?" Charlie asks.

As much as I want to say 'yes', I don't. Charlie doesn't know it yet, but we're going to be voting on letting her go and if the vote is in favor of it, she won't be able to come back.

"We'll see," I say.

Once everything is put away and we're ready to go, I swipe my T-shirt and cut off the bench and head toward the swinging door. Charlie's ahead of me, and she steps through, holding the door open for us with an outstretched arm. When Piston walks past her, he stops and pivots to stare at her wrist. His gaze darts from her wrist to my bare chest and back again.

"Huh, ya both have the same tattoo."

Charlie's face turns scarlet, and she ducks her head. I absently rub my fist against my pec where the simple black infinity symbol is nestled among the vibrant colors of the tattoos surrounding it.

"No they don't," Joker insists as he steps closer to inspect both of us. He points to my tattoo. "See, Fen has the Infinite Motors logo and—"

"Dude, not real comfortable with you fucking staring at my chest."

"Wait." Joker holds up a hand and he narrows his eyes. "I was there when Pony did that logo ink. Now that I think about it, you already had the infinity symbol."

"You don't know shit. You were high as hell that day," I argue.

He's right, though. I already had the symbol, but there's an unspoken rule among the Soulless Kings. No member is to ever get a matching tattoo with a chick. It's dangerous territory and the second it happens, the chick tends to read more into the *association* than is there. Not only that, but since we have an in-house inker, we're not always of sound mind when the needle is vibrating into our skin. No good decision is ever made while high or drunk.

I wasn't drunk when Charlie and I got our tattoos at the local shop. I was stone-cold sober and knew exactly what I was doing. Breaking rules and branding myself as hers.

"High or not, I remember what I remember."

"Hold up," Piston interrupts. "Is that where the name of the shop came from? That damn symbol?"

Charlie's eyes dart to mine at that question. I've never told anyone why I chose the name I did and I don't feel like telling them now, but they're not giving me any other choice so I give a curt nod.

"Why would you do that?" Charlie asks, incredulously.

Through this entire exchange I've kept calm, controlled, but that one question of Charlie's and my control snaps. I pull my T-shirt over my head and put my cut on, covering up the evidence of my decisions, my sins.

"Why the fuck wouldn't I?" I growl once I'm fully dressed. "Dammit, Charlie, you were my world, even after you left, there was a part of me that wished you'd come back."

"Seriously?" Joker asks. "You thought she betrayed you. How could you want her to come back?"

"Because she's everything," Piston answers for me when no words come out of my own mouth. "To him, she's everything."

"This is so fucked up." Joker pulls his shirt over his head and shoves his arms through the sleeves. "She's a Black Savage and you're a Soulless King. I don't know how the hell anything between the two of you ever worked in the past, or if it can work now, but shit. Even I have to concede that you two seem perfect together. In some weird, twisted way, the two of you work even when everything in the universe says you shouldn't."

Charlie's gaze shifts to Joker, and before I realize what she's doing, she launches herself at him. When he catches her out of instinct, air whooshes past my lips as I release a breath I didn't know I was holding and at the same time, my heart cracks.

Don't get me wrong, I'm happy that my brothers are coming around and accepting Charlie, but it means nothing anymore. Not when I know we'll be voting on letting her go.

Not when I know that the vote will be in favor of her going back to the Black Savages. Not when I know that she's still got one foot on that side of the MC line.

How am I supposed to be happy when I know that, in less than twenty-four hours, that feeling will likely be ripped away from me… again?

CHAPTER NINETEEN

The hatred and bitterness he's held for so long oozes from him and spills onto the bed, drowning the peace we've found together.

Charlie

I start to follow Piston and Joker to the clubhouse, but Fender takes my wrist, and I spin toward him.

"Let's stay in my cabin tonight," he says, nodding into the darkness and the trees.

I open my mouth to protest, comment on how I don't think the others would like that or whatever, but I let it go when I identify the serious and maybe even sad expression etched into his face.

I nod and let him guide me to the break in the trees where a small gravel path lies. We walk hand in hand in silence while crickets chirp and leaves rustle from tiny animals scurrying about. I like the Soulless Kings' property more than the Black Savages, I realize. There aren't as many trees there, other than a small section near Leal's house. It's less serene.

Will I ever stop comparing the two?

"You've done really good with getting everyone to accept you."

I turn my head toward Fender and raise a brow that he can't see because he's facing forward.

"I don't know about that." I turn and look straight ahead. "There are still some that won't even look at me."

"Piston and Joker like you… the others will come around."

I don't plan on replying, but I can't prevent the scoff that escapes me. Fender stops walking and tugs on my hand, so I'm forced to do the same and I swivel toward him.

"What was that?" he asks.

"What if I don't care if anyone else 'comes around'? Why does it matter so much? We both know you can let me go at any time if you really want. It isn't like you're going to kill me, so at some point this has to end."

He recoils like I've just slapped him in the face, and it sobers me some. I suddenly regret saying anything at all.

"I know," he agrees finally, letting go of my hand and shoving his into his pockets. "It isn't about getting them to agree to letting you go."

"Then what is it about?"

I know the answer the second the question leaves my mouth, and my face falls at his somber expression. They're his brothers, his family. He wants them to love me because he loves me.

Does he love me?

"Do you want to leave, Charlie?" he asks.

"Would you let me if I did?"

He doesn't answer right away, and it feels like it's taking an eternity with the way my heart pounds in my chest. It's weird and I can't fully understand it myself, but I'm conflicted on which way I want him to answer.

I don't want to leave.

I don't know at what point I realized that today, but it's singed into my brain now, as permanent as a tattoo. I love my family, so damn much it hurts, but I don't belong there. I don't know if I belong here either, but I know I belong with Fender and this is where he is.

I don't know if he loves me, but I love him.

My heart skips when the thought comes into my mind, and I silently scream the words.

I love him.

But how can you love someone who's made you a prisoner?

"Fender, am I free to go or not? No more bullshit with the other brother's opinions. You're the president, you make the call."

"It isn't always my call. Why the fuck can't you get that?" he says with a shake of his head. "We don't do things like the fucking Black Savages."

"So no, I'm not free to go then?"

My chest tightens, even as it mixes with relief. Fuck, this is confusing.

He stares at me another minute, his head tilted to the side as if to study me. With his jaw tense, he squares his shoulders and pulls the key to his bike from his pocket. He fumbles it in his hand a few times before extending it to me.

I reach out and carefully take it, pulling back slowly like I'm waiting on him to change his mind.

"I'll let the guys at the front gate know they're not to stop you."

"Okay," I say, still waiting to see if he'll change his mind. He doesn't blink, the key feels heavy in my hand. *Too* heavy. My hands begin to sweat and become slippery against the metal.

I slip the key into my pocket and shrug when Fender gives me a funny look. "I think I'll hold onto it."

A smile spreads across his face, and he takes my hand again. We walk the rest of the way to the cabin and decide we both need a shower.

I set the key on the bathroom sink and climb into the shower that Fender already has running and is spraying his head. He's facing away from me, and I weave my arms around his waist, hugging myself to his back.

"Are you not going to leave?"

"No," I whisper, the word feeling more like relief than defeat. It isn't me giving into him. It's me giving into myself.

"Why?"

"Because you don't want me to." My voice breaks, despite my determination to keep it even. A string pulls inside me and every bit of strength I have unravels with each tug. Tears burst from my eyes, and I'm thankful for the spray of the shower to hide them.

Fender turns in my arms and hugs me back while I softly cry into his chest. I wonder if he has any idea why I'm crying. If he has any idea how many times I've thought about this, about us being together, and if he has any idea how long I've spent telling myself I couldn't have it. Have him.

"I'm yours, Charlie," he whispers, the words almost swallowed up by the water bouncing off porcelain.

I cry harder and Fender rubs a hand over my back, whispering the words over and over.

"I'm yours."

~

"Favorite color?"

"Green."

"Green?" I ask, raising a brow. "I thought it used to be red."

Fender shakes his head and continues tracing an invisible line on my bicep. We've been laying in bed for hours, catching up on all the things we missed in the four years we were apart and learning some old things that I hadn't known. Like apparently, Fender was on the swim team in high school. He was good, too. Broke the school record for best time.

"Red makes me think of blood ever since..." he trails off, but doesn't pause long before he blinks and is back in the present. "Green makes me think of home. The pines outside and the green after it rains." He lifts his gaze to my face and pins me with his stare. "And your eyes."

I smile at him before looking out the window to see the ferns just outside Fender's cabin. I could get used to this view.

"Your favorite color is still blue?"

"Like the sky on a sunny day."

Fender nods and looks to the ceiling while he thinks of a question to ask me. We've nearly exhausted this game, but it's nice just to talk to him. To laugh with him, smile with him, be with him. If I had known it could be this way, I would've come home a long time ago.

"How did you become president of the Soulless Kings?" I ask, taking his turn but realizing I want the answer. It didn't surprise me at all to see Fender remain loyal to the club he was brought up in, but to see him as the president? It still doesn't feel real.

Fender shifts like he's uncomfortable, and I scoot off his chest. He rolls onto his side and smooths a strand of hair out of my face.

"After you left, our clubs went to war. We're still there, but it isn't quite as brutal as it used to be. We came to a sort of unspoken agreement to stay away from each other until..."

"Until I came back?"

He nods. "During the next six months or so, I became obsessed with avenging my parents, so I spent every waking minute plotting, planning, carrying out counter moves."

"You proved your loyalty," I say, realizing where Fender is going with this. I hate that it's the case, but it makes sense.

Losing everything and filling with hate will give anyone the drive and determination to get where he is.

"And my competence. Prez got sick, and Tiger, our VP at the time, got taken out by a Black Savage. Prez chose me to take Tiger's place. The brothers agreed with him when it was put to a vote. Then when prez died…"

"You were voted to take his place."

Fender's thumb rubs a circle on my shoulder. I take a deep breath and process the information.

"If I had known what would've happened. The war that would've started… Maybe I could've stopped it."

"No one could've stopped it," Fender says with certainty. "When there's that much hatred involved, there isn't anything anyone can do to stop it… Besides, I wouldn't have wanted it stopped."

My eyes narrow and I shift onto my elbow with my head in my hand. "You just said you lost your vice president. You said it was a war."

"It was a war that needed to happen."

"Fender…"

He breaks my gaze and slowly pulls his hand away to rub it over his face. I can see so clearly the war he wages not just with the outside world, but with himself, in his head. The hatred and bitterness he's held for so long oozes from him and spills onto the bed, drowning the peace we've found together.

Fender's wrong. It didn't need to happen. I don't know the details of why it happened and never got the chance to ask my father before he died, but I know it didn't need to happen. It *shouldn't* have, none of it. Maybe it's because I was younger, but I don't remember thinking I could make a difference with the tension between the two families. Now I'm not so certain that's true. I wish I would've stayed to find out…

"Change of subject?" I ask when it's clear we aren't going to agree.

Fender lets his hand fall to the bed and forces a smile that comes off a little too sad.

"Change of subject."

CHAPTER TWENTY

This isn't what I want. It's just what is.

Fender

Bam... bam... bam.

I flinch each time the gavel connects with the wooden surface. My reaction is weak, but I can't help it. I just pray that none of the others saw. If they knew that the war in my head matched the war between us and the Black Savages, they'd send me off to the fucking looney bin. I've always been decisive, calculated, in control. Now, I'm a goddamn mess and all because of a woman I should keep my distance from.

"Settle the fuck down," Piston shouts when the gavel doesn't do it's job.

Voices hush at the demand, and I glance around the table at my brothers. Piston's scowling, no doubt frustrated with the lack of order this morning. Joker's got a lazy smile tugging at his lips, and I can't help but think a Bangin' Betty is responsible for it. Asshole sent out a mass text of a picture of a pair of tits in the middle of the night. After Charlie lectured me about how women should be treated, we got a good laugh. Greaser's leaning on his elbows, a mug of coffee, likely laced with Kahlua, in his meaty hands. Riker's head is tipped back, his eyes closed. I know he's not sleeping, his shoulders are too tense for that to be the case. Flash is staring at the screen of the laptop sitting in front of him, his lips moving as he silently reads whatever words are there. Curly and Burly are at the other end of the table, solemn expressions on their faces.

"Listen up," I begin. "We're all aware of the threat that Leal made against the Soulless Kings. He gave us forty-eight hours to return Charlie, and we've been lucky up until now that he hasn't followed through."

"Luck's got nothing to do with it." Riker lets out a huff of laughter. "They're all a bunch of pussies. They ain't comin' for us."

"That's the kind of thinking that'll end up with a body count... on our side," Piston snarls. "Have you all forgotten the attack four years ago? Because I haven't. And I know your prez hasn't."

Piston's gaze travels to mine, and I give an almost imperceptible nod. He may not always agree with what I do, or more precisely, what my heart wants to do, but he's got my back, no ifs, ands or buts about it.

"We can handle whatever they bring our way," Joker inserts. The lazy smile is gone and in its place is a steely look of determination. "We just have to be prepared."

"And you think we're fucking prepared?" I argue. When they all look at me like that's the dumbest question in the world, I continue. "Because I've got two dead parents that would say otherwise."

"They'll only attack as long as we have their princess." Burly's voice is deep, gravelly from years of smoking, both cigarettes and joints. "I think letting her go needs to be voted on. As much trouble as she's caused and as much as she needs to pay, maybe we can stop things before they even start."

"Agreed," Greaser says. "Don't get me wrong, I get why we

took her and I'm all about this war between the two clubs, but Burly's right. Even if an ambush can't be stopped, letting her go will at least buy us some time."

Conversation among the members heats up, but the underlying tone is agreement about doing what needs done to either stop or slow what we all know will inevitably come, no matter what we say here. This might be what one would call a pivotal moment. My club, my *family*, is coming to the decision on their own to let Charlie go. It should make me happy. Hatred and revenge are no longer the driving force when it comes to her. Why, then, do I only feel a sense of dread? Why is anger searing me from the inside out, and why do I have the sudden urge to run from this place and take Charlie with me?

"Goddamnit!" Piston's fists slam on the table as he surges to his feet. Everyone shuts up and stares at him. "We're getting off topic. I agree, we need to vote on letting our prisoner go."

Joker snorts at the word 'prisoner' and honestly, I get the sentiment. Charlie is no longer a prisoner of the Soulless Kings. I was prepared to let her go last night, vote be damned. She chose to stay. She's here of her own free will, whether they know it or not.

"The Black Savages will come for us. I know that, Fender knows that. Shit, you all know that. This isn't going to just go away, whether we have their princess or not."

"We *don't* know that," Burly argues.

"Jesus," Piston mumbles. "You've been a Soulless King for how long, Burly? Twenty years, thirty? When have the Black Savages ever backed down from a fight? When have they ever not followed through on a threat?"

"There's a first—"

"Stop," I demand and my voice is so loud it seems to echo off the walls. "Don't you get it? They're winning this war right now. Every second we waste arguing about shit is another second they're getting exactly what they want." I scan the room, letting my stare connect with each man at the table. "Every single one of you has a point, but points only count in darts. Points don't mean shit in war. And make no mistake, we're at war. Now what are we gonna do about it?"

"I vote to let Charlie go," Joker says as he stands. "But not just for the reasons everyone thinks."

"Why then?" Curly asks, the hand holding a pen hovering just over his notebook like he doesn't want to get anything wrong in his notes.

"Look, I don't know why the ambush four years ago happened. I don't know if there were forces against us that we don't know about. Hell, I'm still not one hundred percent sure that Charlie had nothing to do with it." Joker holds his hand up when a growl escapes me. "What I do know is that she's not so bad. And our president seems to have a hard-on for her and believe in her innocence. That's enough for me, and it should be enough for all of you."

I'm floored by Joker's little speech, although I shouldn't be. Joker's not a bad guy. Sure, he's unpredictable and a little crazy at times, but he's also loyal as fuck.

"I vote to let Charlie return to the Black Savages." Joker pauses, taking a deep breath and blowing it out through his nose. "And when she's gone, we prepare for the biggest fucking war of our lives because letting her go isn't going to stop a damn thing."

Everyone glances at each other before thumping twice against the table.

"I'd like to take it one step further," Piston says once the voting is over. He looks at me, and his stare holds a hint of apology. "Charlie *has* to go. We've voted to release her, but I think we should also vote to ban her. Temporarily," he rushes to add when I stand up. "Just until we can be sure that the Black Savages aren't going to keep threatening us if she's here."

"We're not voting on that," I say and shocked expressions turn my way. "I'll agree to it. Fuck, I'll even be the one to ride her ass out of here. What I won't do is ban her because that means, based on the Soulless Kings bylaws, that any means necessary can be used against her if she ever steps foot on our property again. I won't bring her back too early, but I won't sign her execution papers either."

Each man at the table thumps their fist twice on the surface. No vote had been pending. No question posed. As president, I was making a call and there was no room for argument. It feels damn good to know they all have my back anyway.

"Moving on to other matters," I say, needing to talk about something else, anything else. "How are things going with Trainwreck and the other prospects?"

"As good as can be expected," Piston responds. "Trainwreck is tagging along on a run tomorrow. Fucker's a little wild, but I think that'll settle in time."

"Let's hope not," Joker laughs. "Crazy will keep him alive."

"What about Jake, Greg and Scott?"

"Let's just say they're adjusting to their road names," Piston chuckles.

"Damn, man, Jake about died when someone called him Royal. He's a rich motherfucker and likes to flaunt it, but we're bringin' him down a notch or two." Flash is trying to hold in his laughter as he recounts how each prospect got their road names. "And Greg? Dude's huge so we call him Tiny. Really screws with his head too cause Squirrel told him it was because he was so big his dick probably looks tiny between his tree trunk thighs."

Now we're all laughing, and damn it feels good. We haven't had prospects in a year or two, and there's something about the normalcy of it that calms me.

"I don't know if I should even ask, but what about Scott?"

"That one's fuckin' weird, that's for sure. Haven't quite

figured out if it's good weird or bad weird." Greaser's laughter dies down and he looks serious. "He keeps going on and on about how he was an Eagle Scout and how that prepared him for MC life. He's now Eagle but I gotta say, not sure he's gonna make it."

"And I thought Trainwreck was bad." I shake my head at the thought of the two prospects that could probably get us all killed if we gave them too much leeway. "Okay, moving on. Anything else we need to discuss today?"

No one stands up, so Piston adjourns church. There are other matters that need discussed—our drug supply, financials from each business—but those can wait. Right now we all need to focus on the Black Savages' threat.

Everyone other than Piston and I file out of the room. When he makes no move to start a conversation, I head toward the door and grab my weapon out of the box. Just as I'm about to walk through the doorway, he calls out to me.

"Hey, Chris."

I freeze at the use of my given name. He hasn't called me that since we buried my parents, and the fact that he's using it now tells me that he's talking to me as my best friend and not my VP.

"I can take Charlie home if you'd rather not. I know how you feel about her, and if I can make this a little easier on you..."

I glance over my shoulder at him. How the hell does he know how I feel when I haven't even admitted it to myself, much less out loud?

"Thanks, Sam." Saying his name feels just as foreign as hearing my own. "I gotta do this, though." He gives a tight nod, and I take a deep breath before turning away from him. Before walking through the doorway, I glance back. "If you really want to help, I've got something you can do."

"Anything."

"Where are we going?"

Charlie's green eyes lit up when I told her we were going for a ride, but her excitement was quickly replaced with unease when I grabbed her shopping bags from the day we took her from the mall. She's looking at me with questions dancing in those emerald depths, and the room threatens to swallow me up.

"I'm taking you home," I say past the lump in my throat.

"But… I don't understand."

"What don't you understand?" I snap, forcing steel into my tone when all I want to do is drop to my knees and beg for her forgiveness. "You were kidnapped, we got what we wanted, we don't need you anymore, end of story."

Her eyes grow round and her fists clench at her sides. She's gearing up for a hell of a fight, and I don't blame her. It must seem like I've done a complete one-eighty. Just last night I told her I was hers and now I'm kicking her out.

"This is a joke, right?" Her foot starts to tap on the cabin floor, and she props a fist on her hip. "You're fucking with me."

"Do I look like I'm joking?" I stalk toward her, wrap my fingers around her bicep and thrust her toward the door. "Let's go."

Charlie plants her feet and yanks out of my hold. Her face is red and her body is rigid. I hate what I'm doing to her, but it has to be this way. If I don't stand my ground, I'll let her talk me into keeping her here and then what? Another ambush? More carnage? At least this way everyone will be safe… or as safe as members of an MC can be.

"You've got five seconds to get your ass out to my bike," I growl.

"Or what?"

Or nothing.

"Four seconds."

She doesn't move.

"Three... two..."

I reach her in two long strides and lift her up to throw her over my shoulder. Her ass sticks up in the air, and she pummels my back with her fists.

"Put me down!"

"Not happening, princess."

I walk outside and ignore her assault. She's stronger than she looks and her strikes hurt, but I deserve every single one. By the time I reach my bike, my anger at her is no longer all an act. She's pissing me off and maybe that's a good thing. It certainly makes this easier.

"I'm gonna put you down and you're going to stand still. Got it?"

She huffs but says nothing. I lower her to her feet but don't let her out of my sight. I don't trust her not to try and run. I could easily catch her, but I'm not in the mood to chase her through the woods surrounding my place.

"I'm not getting on your damn bike." Charlie crosses her arms over her chest, and I have to avert my gaze because the action causes her tits to pop up in a sinfully sexy display of cleavage. "If you want me to leave, fine, but I'll drive myself outta this hell-hole."

On the inside, I wince at her words, but on the outside, I maintain my resolve. If she's mad now, she's going to be fucking pissed when I tell her why she can't ride her own bike.

"Not possible," I mumble as I stuff her purchases in my saddlebags.

"What do you mean 'not possible'?"

I square my shoulders and look her in the eye. "Your bike's not here. I had Piston take it back to your place."

"What the fuck, Fender? You know you can't give him permission to ride someone else's—"

"I did what I had to," I shout, cutting off her censure. She's not wrong. A bike is sacred and no one rides it without the owner's permission. Maybe I crossed a line, but I had my reasons.

"No, you did what suited your purposes."

Charlie's body seems to deflate and her arms drop to her sides. Her face remains red so I know she's still angry, but she's outta gas. We can fight all fucking day and it won't change anything. I don't want her to go, she doesn't want to go, but she *has* to go.

"Just get on the damn bike."

She steps around me and straddles the bike, scooting as far back as the seat will allow. I stare at her a moment before mounting up in front of her and revving the engine. I glance over my shoulder at her and raise a brow. She huffs out a breath and rests her hands at my waist. Not exactly the clinging I was hoping for, but it's better than nothing.

I steer the bike off Soulless Kings' property, and her nails dig into my sides when I pick up speed as we head south on the Coastal Highway. Any other time and I'd pull off to the side of the road and we'd enjoy the views, make out a little, maybe fuck on the back of my bike depending on the time of day. This time, though, the views might as well not exist and there's no sexual tension that's begging to be released.

When I reach Black Savages' property, I slow the bike to a crawl and park in front of their iron gates. Charlie's bike is there, right where I instructed Piston to leave it. I drop the kickstand, and the bike leans to the side a bit. Neither of us make a move to get off of it.

"Is this really what you want?" Charlie whispers. There are tears in her voice, and I die a bit knowing I put them there.

"Does it matter?"

"Yeah, Chris, it matters."

I should tell her 'yes', that this is what I want. I should say whatever I have to in order to make this easier, to make her hate me so she can walk away and never look back. And even though I know what I *should* do, I can't quite bring myself to tell her the lie.

I swing my leg over the seat and watch as she gets off on the other side. We stand there, staring at each other. Her with tears streaming down her cheeks but not reaching her chin before the wind dries them. Me with a knot in my stomach and my heart shattering into a million pieces.

I take a deep breath and say the only thing I can.

"Charlie, I'm yours. I will always be yours." Her lips tip into a wobbly smile, and it makes my next words that much harder. "But I'm a Soulless King and you belong to the enemy. I love you so fucking much, but this isn't about me. Fuck, it's not even about you. It's about honor and loyalty and family. So, no," I take a deep breath and exhale it slowly. "This isn't what I want. It's just what is."

CHAPTER TWENTY-ONE

Love can conquer many things, but it doesn't stand a chance among our rivals.

Charlie

I watch the bike disappear in the distance and then wait for what feels like an eternity before taking my eyes off the road. Tears threaten to spill over, but my jaw is in a hard line.

I hear my father's voice in my head, telling me not to cry, and I listen to it. Last night I cried for all the things I didn't know I could have. Now, I refuse to cry for all the things I can't.

This isn't what I want. It's just what is.

You're right, Fender, I wish I would've said. Instead, I'd just stared at him, my eyes watering even as my teeth ground together and fists clenched. He drove off without either of us saying another word.

I turn toward the iron gate and stare down the long driveway that leads to what I used to think of as home. The houses are so far back, I can't see them from where I'm standing.

Leaving my bike and clothes behind, I climb over the

wrought iron gate instead of buzzing for someone to open it because I'm not sure I can speak past the lump in my throat right now. I could use the walk anyway, anything to prolong the inevitable.

I walk down the dirt path feeling numb. I can feel the wind on my face, but that's all I seem to be feeling. Not abandoned. Not betrayed. Just numb, or maybe resigned is a better word for it. Resigned to the fact that I'm a Black Savage, he's a Soulless King, and neither of those things will ever change. Love can conquer many things, but it doesn't stand a chance among our rivals. We lost.

I lost.

The clubhouse is the first structure down this road, and when it comes closer into view, I see Leal and Mercenary working on their bikes in the front yard. Mercenary sees me first and nudges Leal before pointing.

As soon as our eyes connect, he shoots to his feet and races toward me.

"Charlotte!" he yells, throwing his arms around me and lifting me into the air.

I close my eyes to hold the tears in and wrap my arms around him, burying my face in his shoulder. He smells greasy from working on his bike, but it's distinct from Fender's scent.

He sets me on my feet and holds my face in his hands while he searches me for bumps and bruises. "Are you okay?" he asks, insistently. "Did they hurt you?"

"No." I shake my head.

"Char, we were coming to get you today. We would've come and got you sooner, but we wanted to hit them when they least expected it so we could make sure you weren't heavily guarded. Those fucking animals don't know what they have coming to them."

There's a defensiveness in his tone, almost as if he doesn't want me to think they weren't coming for me. As I look at

Leal's worried eyes and the crease in his brow he gets when he's concerned, guilt filters into me for not calling him to tell him I was okay.

"They don't want a war," I say.

His eyes narrow, and he pulls back. He wraps his hand around my arm and urges me toward the clubhouse. "Let's get you inside and taken care of. You look dehydrated."

"Leal."

He pauses and turns toward me.

"I'm fine, really. They just... had me hang out for a few days. They didn't hurt me, and they let me go so we can all avoid something no one wants."

"*This* is what they want," Leal says, his temper flaring. He checks himself, then takes my arms and looks at me compassionately. "Charlotte, they took you because they're bastards and they want a fight. I'm glad they had the sense not to harm you, but you're one of ours. They can't fucking touch you."

"What are you going to do?"

Trepidation creeps in and I grow more worried watching Leal's gaze turn cold. I don't know why I didn't fear this or how I didn't recognize that this was coming, but of course it is. Of course Black Savages aren't just going to let this go. Just like Soulless Kings wouldn't.

Images of the people I've come to know and love—Widow, Joker, Piston, Margo, Fender—dead on the wooden floor I walked hours ago fill my head and makes me want to scream.

"We need to get you inside, hon."

Now I feel a little faint, so I let him guide me inside and into the kitchen. I hop on the counter and Leal brings me a cold washcloth and a bottle of water. I press the cloth to my head.

When he pulls out a phone, my eyes go wide. "Who are you calling?"

"Your mother. She's been worried sick." He gives me a sympathetic smile then puts the phone to his ear.

I try not to listen as he talks to my mother. I don't want to accidentally hear the lack of relief on the other end of the line or for my suspicion that he lied to me about her worry to be confirmed. It's easier than I think it will be to block out the phone call because I can't stop picturing what happens next, and now it isn't only Fender and his family's dead eyes in my mind, but my own family's as well.

This could get Leal killed. Leal, the man who has helped my family through the death of my father and taken us as his own. The man who welcomed me home with open arms, not once but twice, despite being one of the only ones to do so.

I can't let any of that happen.

When Leal hangs up the phone, I hop off the counter and toss the cloth into the sink.

"Your mom's coming to get you. Do you want to go wait outside? Some of the other brothers are in the living room and would love to see how you're doing, but I understand if it's too much—"

"Leal, I need you to listen to me, okay?"

He raises a brow and leans back on the sink, arms crossed over his chest. "Okay?"

"I don't want any retaliation against the Soulless Kings."

"What?" He shoves away from the counter.

I hold up my hand to stop him before he can begin his protest. This is going to be one of the hardest things I've ever done, and I don't want to lose my nerve.

"Their president, Fender, and I used to have a relationship, back before I left." I take a deep breath and give him a second to process that. He doesn't seem to be able to. Actually, he doesn't seem affected by it at all, but I wave it off as shock. "I was in love with him then, and I went to see if there was anything still there. They didn't take me. I left on my own."

He gives his head a shake and squints so much I can't see his irises. "Maggie—"

"Maggie didn't know Fender was coming to get me. I'm sure, to her, it looked like a kidnapping."

His eyes grow so cold I think they might've frozen over. He glances toward the kitchen window at the sound of tires on gravel, and I follow his gaze to see my mom pulling up in her Jaguar.

Leal turns to me and straightens. He looks so much taller when he's angry. So much more intimidating.

"Tonight, we'll put the Soulless Kings' fate to a vote. I suggest you keep the information you told me to yourself."

He opens the door and gestures outside for me to leave.

"You would still attack them, knowing that it wasn't a kidnapping?"

"I don't think you want to know what would happen if anyone thought it wasn't a kidnapping." He breaks my gaze to look at my mother's car. "Go, Charlotte."

I walk tall past him, but inside I feel as crumbled as I did the day I showed up at my dad's funeral. It's the right thing to do, though, and for that, I believe my dad would be proud of me. It's the only thing I think might stop the attack, and it still might not be enough.

I pause just outside the door and glance at Leal over my shoulder. "They all have a right to know."

His expression doesn't change. He closes the door in my face, and I'm left standing there, as hopeless as when I showed up.

But I'm not hopeless. I can fix this. I just need a plan.

My mother's car purrs behind me, reminding me she's there. I turn and walk to the vehicle and climb into the passenger seat. She's facing me, but I don't look her way.

"You're all right," she states, matter of factly. I don't think she means it to sound so uncaring, and it's more awkward than anything else.

"Yeah," I say, deflating into the seat and mentally running through my options. "I'm all right."

"I'm glad." She places a delicate hand on my thigh, and I spin her way. She looks like she's aged ten years in the last few days, and her hair is a mess. Even with her words awkward and almost sterile, when I see her eyes I can tell this has been hard on her. And I guess I can see why. Not only did she just bury her husband, but she also just lost her daughter after getting her back.

I lean into her shoulder, and she wraps her arms around me and shushes me softly when my crying comes. I'm sure she thinks it has to do with what they did to me, and I want to tell her the truth, that I'm in love with their leader. That I've been in love with him for years and he's the reason I left. That I've been willing to betray my own family for him.

But I don't say those things. The sympathy she's giving me feels too good right now, too right.

After I've calmed down and we've been parked in the driveway for what feels like too long, I lean back in my own seat and Mom puts the car in gear and drives away toward our house.

"Do you want to talk about it?" she asks, her voice soft.

"No."

My voice comes out harsh, and I cringe but don't correct myself. Then an idea comes and I sit up straighter. Leal said they'd be voting on what to do about the Soulless Kings tonight, which means nothing has been decided yet.

They're going to have church. If I can listen in without them knowing, I'll know what they're planning, and I can warn Fender.

The images of bodies laid out on the ground of the Soulless Kings' property fill my head again, and I shiver.

I have to stop this.

CHAPTER TWENTY-TWO

What do I do, mom?

Fender

"Maybe you should slow down, son."

Margo calling me 'son' is like metal grinding on pavement after a bad crash. There are times when I don't mind it because I know she means well, but this is not one of those times. I'm not her son. She's not my mother. That's a title reserved for a dead woman.

Rather than responding or arguing with her, I hold up two fingers to let her know I want two more shots of tequila. She shakes her head and scowls but gets the liquor bottle from under the bar and begins pouring double shots into the glasses in front of me. Before she even has a chance to put the bottle back where it belongs, I'm savoring the fiery path the liquid makes on it's way to my stomach.

"You can't drink her away," Margo says as she wipes down the bar with a rag. She glances at me, and when I make no move to shut her up, she continues. "We don't get to pick and choose who we fall in love with. Believe it or not, this isn't a problem that's unique to you. Shit, it's not even a problem that's unique to MCs. Charlotte Dorn is a—"

The glass that my fingers were curled around shatters against the wall behind Margo. I lean across the bar, bracing myself on slightly bent arms. I was hoping that my outburst would intimidate her, but it's not. Instead, she's got her hands on her hips and is tapping her foot on the hardwood floor.

Goddammit! I can't do anything right.

"Don't you dare say her name," I growl. Margo's eyes grow round, and I whirl around to face the rest of the now silent crowd. "You hear me? The next person to fucking utter that name will be permanently banned from the Soulless Kings."

Murmurs of agreement fill the air. They all know that that's not a decision I can make, not on my own anyway. Permanent banishment is a matter that must be put to a vote, but at the moment, I don't give a damn about rules or bylaws or tradition. I just want the pain to fucking stop.

"Here, Fen." Piston thrusts a joint in my direction.

I stare at it like it's sprouting wings. I want it, the calm it'll bring, but somehow calm is a state of mind that I don't feel I deserve the luxury of. I glare past Piston, toward the others, and my fists clench at my sides when I notice they're all still staring.

"What the fuck are you staring at?" I demand. "Can't a man be pissed off without everyone looking at him with pity?"

Piston pulls his cell phone out of his pocket and taps the screen. The music comes to life around us, and I am grateful that Squirrel connected all of our devices to the Bluetooth speakers so any of us could switch up the tunes when and if we wanted to. Piston scrolls through his music library and stabs the device with a pointed finger one last time before shoving it back in his pocket.

Buckcherry's 'Crazy Bitch' blares from the speakers, and everyone returns to what they were doing. I can't help the upward tilt of my mouth. Bangin' Betties are back to blowing whatever dick is in front of them, and the rest of the crowd is dancing like their lives depend on it.

I grip the end of the joint between my thumb and forefinger and bring it to my lips, drawing hard on it and holding my breath to let the herb take effect. Piston watches me closely, too closely, and I take another puff before passing it back to him. This goes on for a few minutes, this puff puff pass, and then the joint is gone.

"Feel better?" Piston's expression is serious.

"Do you need me to tell you I do?"

"I need you to tell me the fucking truth."

"No, I don't feel better."

"Be right back."

Piston turns and weaves his way through the party, tapping the shoulders of a few brothers as he passes them. When he disappears from my line of sight, I turn back to the bar. Margo is talking to Burly, and his hands are down the back of her pants copping a feel so it takes her a minute to register me staring.

"What can I get you?" She asks and her tone is cool, clipped.

Guilt rushes through me. She was trying to help, and I lost my temper. Not only is that not how we treat women—*our* women—around here. Bangin' Betties are generally treated like the hangaround sluts they are, but a claimed woman? They're treated like the queens they are. Or at least they should be.

"Jesus, Mar," I push out as I thrust my fingers through my disheveled hair. "I'm sorry. I shouldn't have taken my anger out on you."

I duck my head, shame mixing with the guilt. My mother taught me better than that. Hell, so did my father.

"Ya want another beer?"

My head whips up at her question. She's letting me off the hook, and while I know I don't deserve it, I take her forgiveness without another word.

"Sure." I glance at her husband and see the censure in his eyes, the disappointment. I rush to add, "Please."

Margo hands me a bottle of Hop Venom, and just as I'm about to tip it back and take a swig, I'm thumped on the back. I spin around and glare at the prospect, my lips twitching at the nervousness on his face.

"Piston said to tell you church starts in five minutes." Trainwreck stands a little taller and his face becomes a mask.

"What the fuck?"

"He said you'd understand once you got there."

"Anything else?"

"Yeah. He said it's being held at the secondary location. Wherever the fuck that is." That last part is mumbled under his breath, almost as if an afterthought.

"What's that, prospect?"

"Nothin'."

"That's what I thought."

I glance over the prospect's shoulder and notice a girl standing on the opposite side of the room, staring in this direction. She's young, almost too young to be in a place like this, but who am I to judge? I teethed on beer bottles and biker leather.

"Looks like you've got a fan," I say to Trainwreck.

He looks over his shoulder, and when his attention returns to me, his face is a ruddy red. He's blushing and I can't help the snort that escapes. Something tells me that he's going to live up to his nickname in more ways than I could've predicted.

"Ah, that's just Corrie."

"Corrie?" I tilt my head as I try to place the name. I come up empty.

"Corrine Mathers. She's new to town, I guess. I met her at Chuggies, that dive—"

"I know what the fuck Chuggies is," I snap. "Our bar not good enough for you?"

"No, sir. It's just…"

Trainwreck's voice trails off, and I decide to let him off the hook.

"I'm just fucking with you, Trainwreck. Welcome her for me," I say, and I let a little hint of a hidden meaning drip into my tone.

I stalk past him, slapping him on the back as I do. I hear him ask Margo for two beers and chuckle. Looks like the kid is taking my suggestion to heart. I shove the side door open and inhale the fresh air into my lungs. It's a cold night, but that won't matter in a few minutes.

I follow the trail that winds from the clubhouse, through the woods and ends at the secondary location. The fire is already blazing when I arrive, and there are four brothers standing around it, passing a big fat blunt around.

"Calling church to order," Piston says, glancing at each brother before laughing like he just told some hysterical joke.

Joker, Greaser and Riker join in, and before I can stop myself, so do I. When the hilarity subsides, we all stand tall, no doubt thinking about how this 'church' started. The five of us, we're the original five. We're the ones who grew up Soulless Kings. We're the ones who have been loyal our entire lives. We're the ones who, no matter what happens, will never walk away or betray our family. But we're also the ones who carry the heaviest burdens, the ones who sacrifice the most. We're the golden boys of our MC world and the *only* ones who get to participate in this tradition.

"So, boys, why're we having church?" I ask, although I'm sure it has something to do with my foul mood over a certain brown-haired, green-eyed pixie.

"What can we do?" Riker asks, jumping right to the point.

When I glare at him, he scoffs. "C'mon, Chris, it's us. We're not bikers here, just friends."

"I dunno." I shrug before taking a swig of my beer.

"We could go burn their club to the ground," Joker suggests. "Without her in it, of course."

"We could kidnap her again," Riker says.

"We could give the cops an anonymous tip about their drug operation," Greaser chimes in. "Take 'em down without getting our hands dirty."

"Or," Piston draws out the word and focuses his attention on me. "You could just call her. Ask her to come back, be our queen and leave the princess life behind."

My chest constricts at the thought. Leave it to Piston to suggest the obvious, and also impossible. Even if I wanted to ask Charlie to come back, to be my ol' lady, I couldn't. Not after the way I left things. The image of her standing in front of me with a stoic expression on her face as she fights tears enters my mind, and I have to squint to keep it in focus.

"You know no matter what you want to do, we've got your back, right?"

I glance at Joker and note the serious expression on his face. He hasn't exactly been Charlie's biggest fan and he's made that clear to anyone who will listen. But she's started to win him over and it shows.

"I know." I nod as I respond. "I just don't know what the fuck to do."

"Maybe that's not such a bad thing," Riker says.

"How the hell is that not a bad thing?" I snap.

"Think about it. You've always acted on impulse where she's concerned. Maybe this time should be different."

"Go on," I prompt.

"The Soulless Kings and the Black Savages have been rivals since before we were born. A relationship between two of their members should be doomed, but it doesn't have to be. If both people want the same things and love each other enough, anything can work. You just have to want it bad enough and love the other hard enough that the rivalry no longer matters."

"Jesus, when did you become such a Romeo?" Joker chuckles.

"Fuck off, *Brian.*" Riker's use of Joker's given name does the trick. It shuts him up, as it always does because it reminds him that he's just a man, like every other man on the face of the Earth.

"I gotta say, I think Riker's on to something." Piston's expression turns thoughtful.

"For fuck's sake, if you're all gonna get philosophical, at least light up another joint."

Greaser pulls a joint out of his pocket and lights it up. After he takes a hit, he passes it to his right, which unfortunately means I'll be the last motherfucker to get any.

As we stand there, smoking pot and drinking beer, the flames dancing to the music of the night, I tilt my head up to the sky and stare at the stars. My brothers, my *friends,* continue to discuss how I can do things differently this time around, how I can bring Charlie to our side, how we can destroy the Black Savages without bringing carnage to our own doorstep. I know I'm lucky to have these men at my side, but it's not their input I want right now.

I find the North Star and it seems to wink at me, as it always does when I need guidance. The original five may use this spot for 'church' but it's also a place I come to when I need advice from the only woman, other than Charlie, that I've ever loved.

What do I do, mom?

CHAPTER TWENTY-THREE

I lose myself into panic. Lose myself into despair, defeat.

Charlie

The leather of my jacket creaks as I shift into a more comfortable position on the tree I've been leaning against for the last two hours. I shouldn't have worn this. It makes too much noise.

I let my head rest against the trunk, but don't take my eyes off the darkened window a hundred yards ahead of me. The window for the conference room they hold church in. As soon as it glows with light, I'm leaving my hidden spot between a few trees and crouching just beneath it to listen in on the meeting.

This would be so much easier if I knew what time it was starting.

I tap my fingers on my thigh and count back from one hundred as I wait, just to distract myself from the far more disturbing thoughts that have been bombarding my mind while I've been standing here. Like the possibility they already had church, and I'm too late.

Ninety-nine, ninety-eight...

Or the fact that I haven't seen a guard walk the perimeter since I've been here, meaning they've decided our manpower is better spent somewhere else.

Ninety-seven, ninety-six, nin—

Warm light glows in the distance, and I squint to be sure it's coming from the correct window.

Here we go.

I take a breath and plant my foot in that direction, hoping with everything in me that this isn't the time a guard decides to come by. I halt when a crunching sounds behind me, and I spin in a panic to face the source.

My wide eyes narrow when they land on green eyes, so similar to my own.

"Did you at least crack the window first? Their voices will be muffled if you didn't."

My expression doesn't change, but my heart gallops in my chest. She knows. My sister knows what I'm about to do.

What has she told them?

"I'm just heading up to the house to talk to Leal."

Her eyebrow lifts, and she comes closer. "What have you been doing all this time then? Working up the courage?"

"Yes."

She stares at me another moment with her brow lifted, then barks out a laugh and shakes her head. "You're such an idiot, Charlotte."

My fists clench at my sides. "I am not an idiot."

"Yeah? Well, neither am I. I know what you're doing, so just answer me. Did you crack the window?"

She seems like she genuinely wants to know, and it confuses me more than anything she could've said.

Has *she* done this before?

"Yes."

She gives a curt nod and looks out toward the house. "Good."

"Sylvia, what are you—"

"Do you really think you're the only one who's ever thought about being something other than a Black Savage?"

Honestly? Yes, that's exactly what I thought.

I don't answer, and she glances at me before continuing. "I've thought about running too. Not because of a fucking *guy*, but I've thought about it. You really ruined my chances when you took off. Dad became ten times more protective. You may as well have put the handcuffs on me yourself."

I shake my head and try to make sense of what she's saying to me.

This is why she hates me? Not because I betrayed the family but because I took her shot at a different life?

"Sylvia, I didn't know."

"That's because you don't *look*, Charlotte… You and everyone else. Leal was stupid enough to believe your boyfriend actually kidnapped you."

I open my mouth to correct her but think better of it. She knows more than I thought anyone did. No need to point out the one thing she doesn't have right just to have to explain *why* he kidnapped me.

I glance at the glowing light in the distance again.

"Come on, I'm listening with you."

Sylvia starts toward the window before I have the chance to protest, and I follow behind, my head whipping in all directions to look out for anyone guarding the area.

We slow as we make it close to the window and duck beneath it. I press my back against the brick wall and cringe when my jacket squeaks. I can't help but notice Sylvia doesn't make a sound and crouches gracefully in all black, with her ear angled toward the top of the window.

How many times has she done this?

Inside, conversations drown one another out. It's still the beginning of the meeting, so I know I didn't miss the important discussion. Probably the only one they're having tonight.

Finally, Leal's voice is the only one that filters through the window as he tries to regain control over the meeting.

"Quiet! I know you all have something to say, and you'll get your chance. But for now, we need to decide on a time for the raid."

"That bitch isn't worth it!" Someone's voice I don't recognize shouts. I feel Sylvia's eyes move to me, but I don't meet her gaze, nor do I show the hurt that spreads.

Another roar of voices begins. There's a loud thud and I imagine it's Leal's fist pounding on the table.

"Whether she's worth it or not isn't fucking up to any of you!" Leal yells over the angry voices that won't calm even with his demand. They slowly fade as he speaks. "Do you realize who you're talking about right now? She's Dyno's daughter!"

"She's a traitor!"

"She's a Black Savage, and she's family. Her reasons for leaving us aren't clear, but I know she had them…"

His voice trails off as he defends me, and the breath caught in my throat whooshes out. I lay my forehead against the cool brick and breathe in its scent. He didn't tell them about my alliance with the Soulless Kings. He didn't even fucking tell them, and still, they hate me. Simply for not wanting to be a part of them.

No wonder Sylvia couldn't leave.

"Can we at least agree that the Soulless Kings have done us wrong?" Leal asks, sounding almost defeated when the protests won't fizzle out. No one agrees with him, or if they do, they're quiet. This isn't about the Soulless Kings. Whatever Leal says goes, and they all know it. But that doesn't mean they have to be happy about it.

Muttered agreement sounds throughout the room.

"Good. Can we also agree that we aren't going to be pussies and back down from the clear challenge they threw at us by kidnapping one of our own?"

More muttered agreement. They're coming around. My heart speeds up at the angry grunts that filter out into the night air. Leal is getting them fired up, and for what? They might not know the truth, but he does. Why is he doing this?

"Smiley, when are they most vulnerable?"

"Five thirty in the morning, prez," Smiley replies. "That's when their gate security does shift change. The rest of the lazy fucks will still be in bed. They won't know what hit them."

"It's settled then," Leal says and his words are punctuated by a thud that can't possibly be caused by only his fists. "We'll head out at a quarter to five, so I suggest everyone gets some rest."

"What about the specs?" someone asks. "Which members are we taking out?"

"All of them," Leal says, steel in his tone. "We've let these scum live long enough."

The room goes silent as they all process this.

"This time, we leave no survivors."

"Charlotte?"

My sister's muffled voice calls to me, but I can barely hear her past the ringing in my ears. My eyes are trained on brick, but suddenly Sylvia is in my line of sight when my shoulder is jerked back. I look down to see it's her hand that's on me.

"Charlotte, the meeting is over. We have to go."

"Fender," I say, my voice coming out warbled and my lip trembling.

She rolls her eyes and yanks me to stand as she does. I'm still trying to collect my bearings when she pulls me back the way we came, taking no care to shield either of us from the window. I look back and see the light is no longer on.

I pull my hand away, and she stops to glance over her shoulder at me, but I charge past her.

Fender.

Widow.

Joker.

Piston.

Margo.

Burly.

Fuck.

Fuck. Fuck. Fuck.

"There you are, finally," Sylvia says, speeding up beside me with a too-chipper tone. "I thought I'd lost you."

I glare her way then look toward the house before breaking off into a run.

I need to get to my bike. I need to get to *him*.

"Charlotte, slow down," Sylvia hisses, clutching my arm as she runs beside me.

I shake her off.

"You're going to raise suspicions and get us caught!"

With that, I stop. I take deep breaths in through my nose and run my hands over my head.

I turn to Sylvia. "You can't let him die." I grab her shoulders and get in her face. "If anyone stops me from leaving, you have to go to them. You have to warn them!"

"Jesus, Charlotte." Sylvia tries to push me off, but I dig my fingers into her jacket and don't budge.

"Promise me!"

"Okay!"

Sylvia gently takes me hands and pries them from her jacket. There are tears running down my face, but I don't bother brushing them away.

"I promise," she assures me. "He's gonna be okay, Char."

I nod and lift my head to the wind, letting its cold bite dry the drops of weakness. I'm not crying because I'm afraid. I'm crying because I'm about to make the choice to sacrifice my family for this man... again. And I already hate myself for it.

"I know."

Sylvia takes my arm and urges me toward our mom's house. My jaw is hard when we walk up on it and I spot Leal's bike in the driveway. I glance around and note that my mother's Jaguar isn't here, and for that I'm grateful.

Leal is sitting in one of the chairs on the front porch, waiting for us. Sylvia and I say nothing to each other as we approach, but I can see her throwing me worried glances out of the corner of my eye.

"Hey, Uncle Leal," Sylvia says when we get near, no hint of deception in her tone. She's good at this, I realize. I wonder what all she's gotten away with over the years.

"Hi, sweetheart. Why don't you go inside. Your sister and I need to talk."

She moves past me and looks back as she gets to the door. I give her a reassuring nod, and she goes in, letting the screen door slam shut behind her.

"Hey, hon. How are you holding up?" Leal asks me, a sad smile on his face. He's either as good of an actor as Sylvia or he doesn't know we were just spying on them.

I sit in the chair beside him and tuck a strand of hair behind my ear. "I'm okay."

"Good." He plants his large palm on my knee and squeezes. "That's good."

"What's this about?"

"I'm afraid I have some bad news..." He combs his beard with his fingers and sighs like he doesn't know how to tell it to me. He lets his hand drop to his lap. "I've thought a lot about what you told me. How you feel about that guy."

"And?"

"And I realized we don't always get to choose who we fall in love with." He squeezes my knee again, but suddenly it doesn't feel like it's for comfort.

I move my eyes to that hand then back to Leal.

No.

"I remember when I was your age and what puppy love felt like. I get it, Char. I really do."

I scoot to sit straighter and brush his hand off my knee as casually as possible.

I'm reading this wrong.

I *have* to be reading this wrong.

"Uncle Leal, what are you talking about?"

"I'm not angry," he says, that compassionate smile curling his lips. It doesn't have the settling effect it's had on me since I was a little girl. My skin crawls.

"I even tried to convince the others that the Soulless Kings weren't looking for a war. I tried to stop the decision, but you know how the brothers are."

I don't have the words to speak. I can't even call him out on the lie. So much disgust and confusion clouds my brain that I'm frozen in place. Even when he puts his hand on me again.

"You don't need that boy, sweetheart. You belong with a *man*. You belong here… with me." He scoots his chair closer, and my eyes widen when he inhales and closes his eyes.

I should run. I should take this opportunity to slam my palm into his nose, but my brain still won't command my muscles to move and he opens his eyes.

"I can take care of you. That kid never could. Not then and not now."

I shove his hand off of me yet again and open my mouth to tell him to stop this before my fucking ears bleed, but something about the last thing he said stops me in my tracks. The way he said it.

"When I told you I had a history with Fender, you didn't already know about it… did you?"

He chuckles and angles his head. "Sweetheart. You know you've never been good at keeping secrets. Not from me."

"Did you know he would be there during the raid?" My lips part and my chest tightens. "Did you know they would've killed him?"

"Charlotte, listen to me. *He* is the reason you were in danger that day. He put your life in danger then, and he's doing it now. Don't you see that? Don't you see he can't protect you?"

I stand and move back from the chairs until my rear bumps into the porch railing. "You knew I was there that day?" The words come out as a question even though I already know the answer.

He stands too and holds up his hands. "I never would've let anything happen to you, baby. You know that."

"Why didn't you stop them?!"

Tears burst from my eyes, and I throw a hand over my mouth when the reality of it all comes crashing down on me. The real reason for the raid. The reason Fender's parents died. The reason Fender almost died.

"It was you." My words are soft and broken, nearly swallowed up by the wind.

"You needed to see that you can't be one of them. You're one of us. We're stronger than they are. We can protect you. *I* can protect you." He thumps his chest.

"I don't want your fucking protection!"

"Don't say that."

"Did my dad know, too? Did he order people to kill Fender for being my fucking *boyfriend*?"

Leal's eyes darken, and he stands up straight, towering over me like a fucking giant. It doesn't make me feel safe anymore. I'm not the princess protected by guards in the castle. I'm the princess guarded by a fucking dragon so I don't leave the kingdom.

"Your father would never have been so forgiving."

"Then why did he allow the raid to happen? Please," I say,

curling my hands over the rail. If he takes another step toward me I'm hurling myself over and running.

But I have to know this first.

"Please, I need to know."

Leal's face softens like he pities my pain, and it reminds me so much of the way he looked at me at my father's funeral. Back when I thought his eyes were innocent. Back when I thought *he* was innocent.

"Your father was given information that the Soulless Kings were planning an attack on us. So we attacked first."

"And who gave them that information? You?"

Leal doesn't answer, but that's an answer in itself.

"*We* lost lives that day." I shove off the railing out of anger, forgetting that I'm supposed to be keeping my distance. "And how many lives have we lost since because you're a jealous fucking perv?!"

Leal grabs my throat and lifts me into the air. His expression loses any compassionate appearance as he looks me in the eyes, his face hard as stone. I scratch at his hands and struggle, my lungs burning, but he doesn't seem to notice. He peeks over his shoulder into the window to see if anyone is watching.

Sylvia.

I want to scream her name, but air won't go through my windpipe. In or out.

He drops me to my feet and lets me gasp for a few seconds before he presses a hand to my mouth and forces me to look him in the eyes.

"Don't act like you're innocent, Charlotte. I know you killed one of our own that day and you'd do it again for that piece of shit. Only this time I'm not giving you the chance."

A figure comes out of the shadows in my periphery, and I muffle a scream into Leal's hand. It's Donovan, Leal's new VP.

I search Donovan's eyes, but groan when I only see cold

loyalty. Not compassion. Not concern. Only cold loyalty to Leal. We don't teach anything else here.

Leal lifts his hand from my mouth, but it's quickly replaced with Donovan's. I scream and struggle as I'm dragged off the porch, and Leal's compassionate frown returns. He stands there with his shoulder propped against a post watching me.

"I'll be here to forgive you when it's over," he says, his voice sad. Like I betrayed him. Like I should give a *fuck* about betraying him.

I scream and buck and put all of my energy into getting away from Donovan and getting to Fender.

I have to warn him! My brain screams, but all it comes out as is a muffled plea into a dirty palm. I lose myself into panic. Lose myself into despair, defeat.

I lose myself so much that I almost miss it when the curtain in the window behind Leal ruffles.

CHAPTER TWENTY-FOUR

I'm coming, Charlie. Stay strong for just a little while longer.

Fender

"Jesus, I'm coming."

I roll out of bed, intent on breaking the face of whoever is pounding the hell out of my door. As I stumble through my living room, I wonder what time it is. It has to be early based on the darkness just beyond my windows. When I throw open the door, a groan escapes past my lips.

"This better be a fucking emergency," I growl.

"There's a chick at the gate." Craze smiles, but it doesn't reach his eyes. "Says she won't talk to anyone but you."

My first thought is that it's Charlie, and I stand a little straighter knowing I'm going to get to see—

"It's not Charlotte," Craze breaks into my thoughts, and my body tenses with frustration.

"Tell her to come back later," I demand.

I step back so I can close the door, but Craze flattens his palm against it to hold it open. I glare at his hand before glancing back at him.

"Sorry, prez, but she's insistent. Looks scared, too."

"Fuck," I mumble, scrubbing my hands over my face and stepping through the doorway to follow Craze to the gate.

"Ah, prez…"

"What?"

"You might want to put some clothes on."

Craze's eyes remain on mine as he tries not to laugh. I glance down and note that he's right, I'm as naked as I can get. I spin around and trudge to my room to throw on the clothes I discarded on the floor before crawling into bed just a few short hours ago. Once I'm dressed, I grab my gun from under my pillow and tuck it into my waistband. I have no idea who the chick is, but a person can never be too careful.

Craze and I walk to the front gate in silence. It's a long trek, and I can't help but wonder who wants to see me. What is so important that another brother couldn't handle it? When the gate comes into view, illuminated by the moon and the motion sensored security lights, I squint to make out the pacing figure just beyond the black iron.

What the fuck?

"Craze, go wake the others. Tell 'em all to get to the clubhouse."

"Sure thing."

Craze jogs toward the clubhouse, which is at least a half a mile away. I square my shoulders and close the distance between me and my middle-of-the-night visitor.

"You better have a damn good reason for being here."

"Chr—" Sylvia cuts off the word and takes a deep breath. She stopped pacing when I reached her, and now she's standing with her fingers curled around the iron slats of the gate. "I mean, Fender. Can you let me in? Please?"

"No."

I don't know Sylvia, but I've heard enough from Charlie to not like her, not trust her. I stare at her with my arms crossed over my chest.

"You have to let me in!" she shouts, stomping her foot like a toddler throwing a tantrum.

"Yeah?" I shake my head. "I don't think so."

"It's about Charlotte."

My muscles instantly tense, and my mind races through the endless possibilities of why Sylvia would come here about Charlie. None of them are good, but Sylvia is the enemy and I'm not taking the chance that this is a set-up. But I can't ignore her either.

"What about her?"

Sylvia frowns and tilts her head, clearly frustrated that the mention of Charlie didn't immediately grant her entry.

"Do you love her?"

"What kind of question is that? And what the fuck business is it of yours?"

"Answer the damn question, Fender," she snaps.

Anger surfaces at her attitude, but I can't deny that a part of me admires her for it. There are grown men that have smaller balls than she does. I let my gaze roam over her body before returning it to her face to examine her expression. That's when it hits me. She's scared as hell.

"What are you afraid of?" I ask.

"Answer. The. Fucking. Question."

I shake my head at her bravado but let my lips tilt into a grin. Her spunk matches Charlie's, and I realize that I can't lie to her.

"Yeah, I love her." There's a bite to the words. "Doesn't matter though."

Sylvia drops her hands from the bars, and they fall to her sides. She seems to study me for a minute, probably trying to gauge my sincerity, and gives a curt nod.

"It matters. Probably more than you think." Again, she takes a deep breath, blows it out slowly. "If what you say is true, let me in." She stretches her arms out wide. "What am I going to do, huh? I don't have any weapons. You're easily twice my size, so even if I tried, I couldn't hurt you. Just please, *please*, trust me. Do it for Charlotte."

I let her words sink in and realize that she's right. Even if she meant harm, she appears to be alone and I can handle one female with an attitude.

I walk to my right and press a few buttons on the panel that controls the gate. After the combination is entered, the gates slide open. Sylvia's relief is obvious in the way she sighs, and her body seems to deflate.

"Thank you," she says as she crosses over the threshold and takes her first step onto Soulless Kings' property.

"Don't thank me yet. I haven't quite made up my mind what to do with you."

I grip her bicep and tug her along with me toward the clubhouse. Her eyes dart around as we walk, and every once in a while, she stumbles over a rock and I have to tighten my hold to keep her from falling. The silence is deafening, so I try to fill it.

"Does anyone know you're here?"

She shakes her head. "I don't think so. I made sure I wasn't followed. I even parked my car in the woods a few miles down the road and ran the rest of the way here."

Out of the corner of my eye, I see her mouth bow into a smile and it's clear that she's proud of herself. My admiration goes up a notch, but I force it to the back of my mind. Just because she seems to be athletic doesn't mean she's not sneaky. In fact, her own words prove just how sneaky she can be.

"So Charlie doesn't even know you're here?"

"She's the one that told me to come. Made me promise."

"I don't understand."

Sylvia heaves a giant sigh and digs her heels in, forcing me to stop and face her.

"Look, I know how this shit works. You're taking me to the clubhouse and the rest of the gang is gonna be there. You don't trust me, I get that. But I've got news for you buddy. I don't trust you either." She crosses her arms over her chest. "Charlotte, for whatever reason, does. I'd prefer to only go through the details once, so can we please save the interrogation until your little friends are present? Huh? Do you think we can do that?"

"Anyone ever tell you that you've got a fucking smart mouth?"

"All the time."

"Let's go."

I don't grab her this time, instead I start walking and let her make the choice to proceed. I still don't quite trust her, but it took guts to come here alone, and for whatever reason, I'm confident she'll follow me. She clearly has information for me, and according to her, she jumped through hoops to get here.

When we reach the house, Craze is standing on the porch along with Piston and Joker. The smell of weed wafts through the air, and smoke curls from their mouths.

"Everyone here?" I ask as I ascend the steps.

"Yep," Piston responds as he holds the joint out to me.

Before I can take it, Sylvia reaches out and snatches it from Piston's fingers. We all stare at her, wide-eyed, as she draws on it deeply and holds in her breath. She takes another hit before passing it to Joker.

"Damn, that's some good shit. Much better than what we get."

"It's our own special blend." Joker's mouth slams shut as if he realizes too late that she's supposed to be the enemy.

"No worries, guys. Your secret's safe with me." She punctuates her statement with a wink.

The longer I'm with this girl, the more confused I get. I want to hate her. I want to send her packing and go back to bed. But I also want to know why the hell she's here and that won't happen if she leaves.

"Let's get inside." I open the screen door and step through.

When we enter the meeting room, Piston, Joker, Craze and I deposit our weapons in the box before going to our normal seats. I glance back at Sylvia. She hasn't moved, but her gaze is darting around the room. I raise my brows at her and cross my arms over my chest. She may think I'm stupid, but I'm not.

"Oh for the love…" She bends over and pulls a butterfly knife out of her right boot and a pair of pink brass knuckles out of her left boot, depositing both in the weapons box before straightening. "Happy?"

"Not even a little bit," I snarl. "Just get to the reason you're here so we can all go back to bed."

Sylvia walks the rest of the way into the room and stands next to me. I don't know how it works in her world, but only one person stands at the head of the table: me. I let it go because I need to know why she's here and I don't want any more delays.

"Short version… Charlotte's been taken by one of our own, on Leal's order, and she made me promise to come here and warn you about an attack that's planned before the sun rises."

"Wait," Greaser speaks up. "Isn't Leal your president?" When Sylvia nods, he continues. "So you want us to believe that Charlotte's in danger from her own family, and out of the goodness of your heart, you're here to deliver a warning?"

"That about sums it up."

"That doesn't even begin to sum shit up." Sylvia's head whips toward me, and I let my head fall back while I silently count to ten to calm myself down. "I may regret this, but give us the fucking long version."

"You got it," she quips. "Earlier tonight Charlotte and I… *overheard* our boys in church." Sylvia glares at Joker when he

179

snorts at her description of their eavesdropping. "I don't think Charlotte's ever done that before, but I have. Many times. Tonight was different though. Leal, the nutless douchebag, wants war."

"That's nothing new," Piston says when she pauses. "Soulless Kings and Black Savages hate each other. Always have."

"You're not wrong, but this is more than that. It's personal for him."

"Why?"

"Because he's the only one who wants this war. Hell, it's not even a war. It's a full-on murder spree and you're all the target." Sylvia glances at me. "Well, you're the target and everyone else is collateral damage."

My blood boils at the information, burning me from the inside out. My muscles tense, and I have to force myself not to lash out.

"What's this got to do with Charlie?" Piston asks, his tone deadly.

"Apparently Leal knew about their relationship all those years ago. The attack back then," Sylvia pauses and looks at me. "The one where your parents were killed... Leal orchestrated it. He wanted to take you out and claim Charlotte as his own."

"Where is Charlie now?"

"After church, Charlotte and I went back to the house, and Leal was waiting on the porch. He sent me inside, but I guess he didn't realize that the window was cracked open a bit. I ducked down and listened to what he had to say." Sylvia shudders as she recalls what happened. "I gotta say, I kind of suspected that he had a thing for her, but it's so much more demented than a little crush. He thinks she belongs to him."

I bring my fists down on the table, and Sylvia jumps beside me. "She belongs to me."

"Yeah, I know," she says, swallowing hard. "I'm not the enemy here. I don't give a damn about rivalries. Despite the fact that we haven't always been close, I just want Charlotte to be happy. And I want her safe. But she's not right now. Leal has her and who knows what he'll do to her. You need to go get her."

"Do you know where he's got her?" Riker asks.

"He had Donovan, the most loyal of the Black Savages, take her. I watched when they left so I could see which direction they went. Leal stayed behind on the porch for a few minutes but when he left, he went in the same direction. I think they've got her at his house, but I can't be sure. We've got a holding building, but that's in the opposite direction. There's an outbuilding near Leal's house so I'm guessing they're at his place or the outbuilding. Either way, I doubt it's still just Leal and Donovan guarding her now. Most of the Black Savages don't want a war with you guys. They just want to belong to the club and live their lives, but there are a few that are loyal to a fault. Those few will be with him."

"Do you happen to have specs for any of the locations?"

Sylvia shakes her head. "But I can get someone to help who does. Like I said, most don't want a war and they won't be happy when they find out that Charlotte's in danger. She's not everyone's favorite person, especially since she left, but she's one of us. She's family."

I step around Sylvia and walk to the desk in the corner of the room. I yank open one of the drawers and pull out a burner phone to carry back to her.

"Here, call whoever it is you think we can trust." She stares at the phone a moment before trying to take it. I tighten my grip and give her a warning. "If you're playing us, if I suspect for even a fucking millisecond that this is a setup, it'll be your safety that will be in question. Got me?"

"Yeah, I got it."

I let go of the device and she dials a number before putting the phone to her ear.

"Speakerphone," I demand.

Sylvia obeys and while the phone rings, I pray that whoever she's calling will answer in the middle of the night.

"Yo," a deep male voice comes through the line.

"Snow, it's Sylvia."

"Do you have any idea what time it is, Syl?" he asks around a yawn.

Sylvia glances at the phone before responding. "Damn, sorry. I didn't realize it was two in the morning. It's been a long night."

"Whaddya need?"

"I need you to come to the Soulless Kings' compound."

"Jesus, how'd they get ya? Are you okay?" Snow seems a little more alert now that he thinks Sylvia's been taken.

"I'm fine, Snow, but Charlotte's not. She sent me here, and we need your help. Can you do that? Can you come here so we can help her?"

"What're ya talking about? I saw Charlotte a few hours ago and she was fine. She and Donovan were taking a walk."

"Snow, listen to me. Charlotte isn't safe with him. Please, do this for us. Do this for me."

There's a hint of something in her tone that has me rolling my eyes while we wait for his response. Pussy. It gets us all into trouble, doesn't it?

"Shit, yeah, I'll help." There's a rustling noise and it sounds as if Snow is getting out of bed. "I'll be there in a half hour."

"Thanks, Snow."

"You bet."

The call ends and Sylvia hands the phone back to me.

"Now what?" she asks.

"Now, we wait for Snow and we start brainstorming." I glance around the table, making eye contact with each of my men. "Go get yourselves some coffee and wake the fuck up. It's gonna be a long night."

They all file out of the room, grabbing their weapons as they do. Sylvia stays behind and hops up on the table.

"Thank you, Fender."

"Save your thanks for when we have Charlie."

"Right."

I walk to the window, leaving Sylvia behind me. She's earned my trust, for now. As I stare out into the darkness, the moon illuminating the trees in the distance, I picture Charlie the last time I saw her, standing across from me as I pushed her from my life.

I'm coming, Charlie. Stay strong for just a little while longer.

CHAPTER TWENTY-FIVE

You fucking believe me now?

Charlie

The bed creaks from Donovan's shifting, but I don't look at him. I'm tied in a wooden chair on the other side of the room, and even though I'm facing him, my eyes are trained on a framed photograph sitting on the nightstand. I can't look away. No matter how badly I want to, I can't. Because the photo is of me.

I remember the day perfectly. It was my fourteenth birthday and Daddy had just given me a new bike. A *real* bike, not just a little Kawasaki. Dixie is what I called her. She was the smaller version of the Harley I bought when I was seventeen and still ride to this day.

In the photo, I'm straddling the bike and smiling up at the camera, showing off my braces. My hair is in two messy braids that hang past my chest, and my spaghetti straps hang loosely on my shoulders.

This is the photo my father's best friend chooses to keep on his nightstand? What story does he give when people ask about it? What do they think? If I had seen it yesterday, before I knew what I know now, I would have thought it odd but shrugged it off.

Now I can't. Now my stomach turns as I stare at my younger self, full of innocence, and wonder how old I was when he started thinking of me as his.

I wiggle my wrists and cringe at the sting it causes.

"You should stop struggling. You're gonna cut yourself, and then Leal's gonna fucking pummel me."

Donovan's voice is like gravel crushing my ear drums, and I tell myself that's what's causing me to wince. Not the blood running down my wrists from the too-tight zip tie. I've been working it for hours according to the clock on Leal's bedroom wall, and it hasn't loosened any. Maybe Donovan is right. Maybe it is pointless. Maybe I need to figure out a different tactic.

"Why would Leal pummel you when he's the one who had you tie me up?"

"He just doesn't want you running to your boyfriend and fucking everything up. He's made it clear to everyone that you're untouchable."

"Why do you think that is, Donovan?" I ask, careful with the accusation that tinges my words. I don't want to come out and accuse Leal of anything. I'd rather Donovan figure out what Leal is doing on his own.

He doesn't say anything, and that makes me question if he already knows.

Does *he* think the picture's weird?

Finally, I'm able to drag my eyes from the frame to him. He isn't looking at me though. His phone is in his hand and he stares down at it.

"What are you looking at?" I ask, and he glances up at me briefly.

"How the fuck did you do it?" he grits through his teeth. He stands abruptly and fists the phone tightly in his hand, never taking his eyes from it. He walks to me, and when we lock eyes, the fury in his sends confusion clouding my mind.

"Huh? How the fuck did you tip him off?"

He grabs my hair and yanks my head back as he stands over me.

My eyes narrow, and I jerk my head to get out of his hold, but I only manage to make my scalp burn. "What the fuck are you—"

The answer hits me before I even finish the question.

Fender.

He's here.

Oh thank fuck.

Donovan's phone buzzes and he releases me to answer the call.

"How much time do we fuckin' have?" he barks into the cell, turning away from me.

His volume is turned down low enough that I can't hear the answer, but I strain to try anyway. All I can make out is a muffled voice.

"No, I swear to God the bitch has been in my sights this entire time. There's no way—"

Donovan pauses and his head tilts to look up at the ceiling as the person on the other line speaks. He nods like he agrees with what they're saying, but the muffling hasn't stopped. When it finally does, he gives a more forceful nod as if they're here. "Yeah, all right. We're leaving now."

He clicks off and turns to me.

"Uh oh. Someone spoil your plans?"

"Shut the fuck up," he mutters. He walks to Leal's nightstand and ruffles through a drawer, searching for something.

My momentary relief that Sylvia must've gotten to Fender and warned him fades as the seconds tick by. What did she tell him? What do they have planned?

I don't want a fucking war. Not on Soulless Kings' property and not here.

"Donovan, listen to me." He finds what he was looking for and holds up the knife before nudging the drawer shut. My heart stops for a brief moment, but I push on as he walks over to me.

"They don't want a war. Trust me, they don't and they never did. They didn't take me to send a message to the Black Savages. They took me because—"

"Shut the fuck up already!" Donovan yells, spittle flying from his mouth. He steps around me and jerks my arms up, straining my muscles. My face contorts with pain, but I don't allow myself to groan. "No one gives a shit about you except for Leal. I don't care why they took you. They're bastards and they deserve what's coming to them."

"What's coming to them?" I ask as he cuts the zip tie around my wrist. Panic spreads through every inch of me. "What's going on? I can't do anything about it, so just fucking tell me!"

He jerks me from the chair, and I stumble with my ankles still bound. "I'm taking you someplace else in case our location has been compromised. After the fuckers dropped you off, Leal set up sensors a few miles down the road, so we have plenty of time before your little boyfriend gets here on foot." He comes around to my front, and a deviant smile slowly fades from his face. "How the fuck did you get Snow on your side?"

"What?" My eyebrows crease and he dips his head so close to me I want to spit.

"Snow left hours ago and no one knows where he went. Now all of a sudden we're picking up more bodies coming this way. How the hell did you get him to betray his own brothers? You fuck him or something?"

Snow. I have to think hard to even remember who that is, and when I do I realize what happened. His real name is Steven, and he's Sylvia's age. He was a prospect when I left and didn't have a road name. She must have called him.

Did he know about the sensors? Do they know they'll be walking into a trap?

Shit.

"No, I didn't fuck him. I'm in love with the Soulless Kings' president."

He rolls his eyes and crouches to cut the zip tie around my ankles. "Whatever."

"Think about that for a second, Donovan. Think about Leal's motivation in all this. You said it yourself, he's the only one who cares about me, so what's the point in all this?"

"They're coming to attack us right now, you dumb bitch!" He flails the hand with the knife, and I wonder if he realizes how vulnerable he is crouched in front of me while my hands are free.

"No, they're coming to save me from Leal! Look at what you're doing, you idiot! Leal tells you to seek revenge for them holding me hostage, and now you're doing the same thing."

"Because you're Dyno's daughter, and Leal is sentimental."

"No, it's because Leal is a *sick fuck* and wants to eliminate his competition."

"You're a fucking liar, now shut the fuck up!"

I stare at the vein popping on his forehead and wonder if I look the same. This is going nowhere.

He works at the zip tie, and I wait with my muscles coiling. All I need is for him to drop the knife and then...

And then what?

I'm not killing another one of my father's brothers.

But what if I have to?

The zip tie comes loose, and I choke, holding still instead of jerking my knee forward like I intended.

I won't kill again.

Donovan stands and my moment is gone. My heart falls into the pit of my stomach, and I close my eyes.

He tries to usher me forward, but I jerk away from him and take a step back.

"Hey, we're leaving whether you fucking want to or not."

I step behind the chair and shake my head. My hands tremble at my sides. "I don't want anyone else to die. I can't be the reason for it."

"Then choose your boyfriends more wisely. Let's go."

I continue to back away until I hit the wall. Donovan tucks the knife into his jeans and growls as he advances on me. I feel pathetic as he does, like I'm a cornered animal. He looks at me like I'm one too. But like any animal backed into a corner, as soon as his hand touches me, I strike.

My knee lifts and connects with his groin without me having to think about it. His eyes grow comically round, and I'm not sure if it's out of pain or surprise, but I don't waste time trying to figure out which.

My fight instincts kick in, and I clench my jaw as I jab him in the neck just like Uncle Leal taught me when I was younger, and I laugh maniacally at the irony of it as he falls to the ground. I kick at him a few times to make sure he'll stay down, and then I snatch the knife from his jeans, and then his gun. I empty the clip and let the bullets rain down on his body before shoving the gun into my waistband.

"No one else is gonna die," I say, although I'm not sure if I'm actually talking to him. I turn and go to leave the room before he recovers and chases after me, but that picture comes into my view again, and I can't force myself to leave without it. It feels too wrong here.

I go to the frame and yank off the back of it, tossing it to the floor. I go to grab the picture, but my brow furrows when I notice there's two in the frame. I peel back the photo behind the one of me on my bike and flip it around so I can see it.

My stomach bottoms out, and then the nausea follows a second later.

My lips part and my hand flies to cover my mouth as the image of the sleeping girl has a chance to register fully. The sleeping girl is me, around the same age as I am in the first picture, only in this one I'm not smiling at the camera. I don't know it's being taken, and I have no memory of how I could've ended up naked on the familiar couch I recognize from Leal's living room.

I wanted to know at what age he saw me as something other than his niece.

Now I have my answer.

Disgust turns to rage, and as much as I want to rip the photo to shreds, I clutch it tightly in my hand and storm back over to Donovan. He's standing up by the time I get there and he's pissed as hell, but he also looks confused that I'm coming back toward him.

He goes to open his mouth, but stops as I shove the photo at his chest.

"You fucking believe me now?"

CHAPTER TWENTY-SIX

The Soulless Kings might not be the most respectable humans on the planet, but none of us would dare stoop to the level that Leal did.

Fender

"Ya need to hurry it up."

Snow is whispering, and while it's infuriating because it doesn't match the tension swirling around us, I get it. Sound travels and voices carry so we can't take any chance that our position will be determined by our talking.

"Are you sure about this?" I demand, louder than I intended.

"'Course I'm sure." Snow twists to glance over his shoulder at Sylvia. "I hope you're right about all this."

"I am," Sylvia snaps.

We'd tried to force her to stay behind at our compound, but she'd refused. Turns out she not only looks like her sister and has an attitude to match, but she's also just as stubborn and at times infuriating.

When Snow arrived, we'd given him ten minutes to get us

up to speed on the layout of Black Savages' property and buildings. Surprisingly, he also gave us information about the security system and where different guards would be posted.

I hold my arm out to stop everyone from continuing. We decided to bring as few people as possible because our focus is to get Charlie out, not bring down the entire MC. That'll be next. Piston, Joker, and Riker are the only brothers I brought with me, but the four of us are a hell of a team.

"Listen up," I start, whispering this time, although it's gruff. "We're here to get Charlie. We do what we have to do, but we don't forget the mission. Got it?"

"As long as I've got your permission to kill a motherfucker if necessary, I'm good," Joker grates out.

Piston and Riker look at each other and then back to me before nodding.

"Can we cut the bull? Let's go."

Snow steps around me, and it takes every ounce of self-control I possess to not grab his arm and yank him back. I may be an MC president, but I'm not his.

"We better get goin' boys," Sylvia chortles as she follows Snow, slapping my back as she passes.

"Jesus Christ," I mumble.

We follow the two through a gap in the fence line. It's shocking to me that the gap even exists because we've passed plenty of fence that seems to have been reinforced recently. This shit would never happen on Soulless Kings' property. Think Fort Knox, MC style. If you don't protect what's yours, you have no business getting pissed when the enemy strikes.

We silently weave through the trees, and I can't help but wonder why Leal's house is so hidden. My own cabin isn't exactly out in the open, but I didn't make a point to close myself off like Leal seems to have done. What's the point? You're the president, you're supposed to be accessible, unless you're doing something shady.

Snow stops in his tracks right at the edge of a line of trees and turns to face us. "This is the end of the line for me. That's Leal's place." He hitches a thumb over his shoulder to indicate the structure about a hundred yards behind him. "I'd say you'll have two minutes max once you move past me. He's got a silent alarm that's triggered whenever anyone steps foot within a certain distance of his place."

"What?" Sylvia sounds worried, and I wonder why. Has she done more snooping around than just listening in on church?

"Leal's paranoid and controlling. Your dad never would have pulled this shit."

With those parting words, Snow takes off at a jog and doesn't look back.

I take a deep breath and stare at the windows of the structure ahead of us. The place is lit up like a goddamn Christmas tree which isn't necessarily a good thing, despite it providing us with a clear path. I eject the clip from my weapon and assure myself that it's full, for what feels like the millionth time since we left our clubhouse. The others do the same and within seconds, we're off to finish this.

"I wouldn't go any further if I were you."

I whirl around at the sound of the voice and stare at the shadowy figure standing thirty yards or so behind us.

"Yeah, why's that?"

Leal raises the gun in his hand and slowly walks toward us. Piston, Joker and Riker all raise their weapons and point them at his head. I leave mine at my side, although I'm itching to point it and pull the trigger. Leal would look really fucking good with a blood dripping hole between his eyes.

"Because if you take another step, it'll be the last you ever take." Leal glances at Sylvia and smiles. "Sweetheart, why don't you go inside? Donovan will—"

"Donovan ain't gonna do shit, you sick fuck."

I turn around at the addition of a new voice, and standing

on the porch, with a man I've never seen, is Charlie. It's hard to tell if she's hurt, but her head is held high and the smirk on her face tells me enough. She may not be free from injuries, but she's fucking pissed.

"Well, isn't this turnin' into quite the party?" I don't let my gaze waver from Charlie, even though my words are not directed at her. "You hurt, babe?"

"Nothing a little of your TLC can't fix," she purrs and pride swells in my chest. Even with guns drawn, she's pushing buttons like the MC badass she is.

"What the fuck is going on, Donovan?" Leal demands. "Get her back inside and tie her back up!"

Apparently, 'tie her back up' are the words it takes to make me get this party started. I look from Charlie to Donovan, quickly gauging the situation and when Donovan gives a curt nod, I turn around, raising my weapon at the same time, and pull the trigger.

Charlie's scream pierces the air, and she races from the porch to Leal's side. He's not dead, but he won't be walking anytime soon. Blood blooms from his knee and stains his jeans. He's writhing in pain while simultaneously cussing at me, and all I can think is how pathetic he is.

Charlie seems to assure herself that Leal will live before she stands up and advances on me with a scowl on her face. My boys move out of her way, almost mimicking Moses parting the goddamn Red Sea. Sylvia is laughing beside me, and if I hadn't seen her determination earlier, I'd think she was losing her mind.

"What the hell did you do that for?" Charlie demands, stabbing a finger at my chest.

"He was pissing me off," I say casually as I shrug. Too casually judging by the frown on her face.

"He was… Are you fucking kidding me?"

"Ah, no."

"How many more people have to die before this craziness stops? One, five, fifty? How many lives need to be taken before you all realize that you don't have to be enemies?"

"Char, calm down," Sylvia says.

"I will not calm down." Charlie starts to pace back and forth in front of me. "This all started because of me, so I'm putting a stop to it. Right here, right now."

"Babe, you know that's not how this works." I reach out and grab her hand to stop her. "You're mine, and I fight for what's mine."

"That's funny because that's not exactly how I remember it. Or are you forgetting that you dumped me here when you got the answers you wanted?"

"I didn't dump you here," I growl.

"Oh no? What would—"

"While this is entertaining as hell," Joker interrupts. "Can you two save your lovers' spat until later? I'd kinda like to get outta here before we've got more than we can handle on our hands."

"Agreed." Piston turns in a circle, taking in the darkness surrounding us. "Although, I thought we'd have had more company by now. Your club really sucks." He directs that last statement at Leal.

"Shut up!" Leal yells from the ground.

"No one else is coming." Donovan shoves his hand in his pocket and pulls out what appears to be a piece of paper. He walks down the steps and thrusts it at me. "I sent out a mass text of a picture of this." He looks over his shoulder at Leal. "You've got no one in this with you anymore."

I take the paper from his hands and realize it's a photo. It's dark as hell out, but the light shining from the windows lets me make out enough of the image and when I do, my fury builds to an almost intolerable level.

"What is that?" Leal demands from behind me.

My body stiffens, and I shove the photo in my back pocket. I glance at Charlie, and her face has lost some of its color. When I don't respond to Leal, Donovan stomps past me and bends to lift his president up by his cut.

"You don't fucking deserve to call yourself a Black Savage. You don't deserve to call yourself a man."

"You won't get away with this. I'm your president."

"Not anymore, you're not." Donovan throws Leal back to the ground and turns to me. "I don't like you, Fender. Hell, I'm not even a big fan of Charlotte, but I don't condone what's in that picture."

"It's just a damn picture!" So he knows exactly what Donovan handed me. "She's my—"

Charlie whirls around on Leal and stands next to his head, staring down at him. "I'm not your anything. I might fight for there to be less death and bloodshed, but I won't fight to stop your suffering." She crosses her arms over her chest. "Don't make me regret letting you live. Don't push me."

"If your daddy could see you now," Leal taunts her.

"If he could see her now," Sylvia interjects. "He'd be so fucking proud."

Charlie and Sylvia exchange glances mixed with pride, confusion, frustration and sadness.

"Let's wrap this up," Donovan says. "I need to go fill everyone in, and it seems we need to vote on a few things."

"You can't hold church without—"

Donovan smashes his boot into Leal's skull, and his head whips to the side before he collapses, unconscious.

"We're taking him with us," I say, not really sure how the statement will be received.

"Suit yourself," Donovan shrugs.

"Fender, I wasn't kidding." Charlie steps up to me, her eyes pleading. "No more death."

"Babe, I can't promise that. But I do promise that when it's his time, I'll try and make it quick."

"That's the best you're gonna get, Charlotte," Donovan announces, clearly aware of what's likely to take place. "You grew up in this world. Life isn't guaranteed, and sins have to be punished."

Charlie shakes her head and turns to walk toward the woods I walked through earlier.

"Where are you going?" I shout after her.

"I'm going to your bike," she yells without turning around. "I'm assuming you came on it."

I chuckle, as do my boys and Donovan. Sylvia laughs, too, and takes off after Charlie.

"We've got a van up at the main garage. You're gonna need a way to transport him to your property." Donovan spares a glance at his president—former president—and shakes his head. "Follow me."

He takes off in the opposite direction than Charlie went. I order Riker and Joker to follow him and meet us at the road where the bikes are parked. Piston and I make our way to that spot, each of us dragging Leal by an ankle. We're not bothering to watch what's in our path, the more damage done to Leal's body, the better.

"What was in that picture?" Piston asks after a few minutes.

"You don't wanna know," I mumble.

Shit, *I* didn't want to know. It's an image I wish I could unsee. The Soulless Kings might not be the most respectable humans on the planet, but none of us would dare stoop to the level that Leal did to get the photo.

"Tell me this," Piston says. "Are the Black Savages really going to let us get away with this because of it?"

I think about his question. On the one hand, Donovan could be using whatever means necessary to take over the power of the club and the attack that Sylvia warned us about will still happen. The image of a much younger Charlie, sleeping naked and unaware of the depravity around her, enters my mind. On the other hand, if any Soulless Kings member had been caught with that kind of photo, letting them go to the rival wouldn't even come close to the wrath they would experience.

"Yeah, they are."

CHAPTER TWENTY-SEVEN

It's never easy to choose between family and the person you love, and no one should ever have to.

Charlie

I stare at the monitor for the Nightmare Room with narrowed eyes, my arms crossed over my chest. Leal is in there, tied to the same chair I was tied to. He woke up about an hour ago. His blood drips onto the concrete floor, but less so now that he's stopped thrashing.

I hear footsteps behind me and know they belong to Fender when his scent fills the tiny space. I breathe in deeply, and my eyes slide closed when he lays a hand on my shoulder.

"You know putting you in there was the hardest thing I've ever done."

"Was it?" I flinch at the sound of my own voice. There's too much hurt laced in with the hardness. Too much regret.

But I don't regret any of it.

I open my eyes when I realize this, and even with Fender's heavy hand resting on me, a weight lifts off my shoulders.

For so many years, I've been plagued with regret and sorrow, but today, that ends.

I don't know what would've happened if I hadn't left. I don't know where I'd be if I hadn't pulled the trigger on one of my own. I don't know where I'd be if Fender hadn't taken me and put me in that dark space I'm staring at now. But I do know I wouldn't be here.

And *here* is exactly where I want to be.

Fender bends down and sighs into my neck before kissing me there. "Do you think you'll ever be able to forgive me?" he asks, his tone reflecting that same hurt.

I turn around, forcing my eyes away from the man who I no longer think of as an uncle. He's no longer anything.

I wrap my hands around Fender's neck and lean onto my tiptoes. "I already forgive you," I say, pressing my lips to his.

His tongue dips in my mouth, and I moan at his taste. He cups my thighs just below my ass and lifts me into the air before pressing me against the wall. The cold seeps through my shirt and is in direct opposition to my heating core.

Our kiss grows rough and hungry, and we stay this way for several minutes, forgetting about everything else for a short while.

Fender eases away first, and I whimper in protest. He plants several kisses on my neck as he slowly lowers me to my feet.

His eyes drift to the monitor, and I know what he's thinking.

It's time to end this. To end this war and to end this phase of our lives, and I know what it'll take to make that happen.

Just one more death.

"Can you forgive me for this, too?" he asks, looking at me seriously.

I take a minute to answer, staring into the thunderstorm brewing in his eyes. Finally, I give a single nod, and Fender lets out a breath he must've been holding.

He bends down and kisses me before turning toward the door to the Nightmare Room.

"Fender?"

He looks over his shoulder at me.

"Make it quick, okay?"

He nods and turns back around, pressing a button for the lights to come on before he unlocks the door.

And then he's gone, he and Leal now both visible on the screen.

~

Fender

Make it quick.

Charlie's words echo in my head as I stalk toward Leal. I clench my fists at my sides as I realize that making it quick might be the one thing I can't do for her. I fucking hate Leal and the hell he's put me through, put my family through, put Charlie through. He doesn't deserve a fast death.

The minimal amount of blood dripping from Leal's body is hardly satisfying. His clothes are stained with it, both from the shot to his knee and the beating he got from Piston before he was thrown into the van back at Black Savages' property. I ache to make him suffer, but there's one thing I need to do first.

I pull my cell from my pocket and tap the Facetime icon so I can dial a number I hope I don't have to use often.

"Is it done?"

"Just getting started," I reply as I flip the phone around and stick in Leal's face so he can see the screen.

His eyes are swollen, but not so much that I can't see them widen when he sees who I called.

"You got anything to say?" Donovan sneers.

When he'd first answered, I could see the wall of Black

Savages' brothers that stood behind him. It seems that none of them wanted to miss out on this. There'd been hushed conversation at first, but now, other than Donovan's voice, there's a deadly calm coming through the line.

"You're making a huge mistake," Leal says, lacking any conviction. Even he doesn't believe the words coming out of his mouth.

"The only mistake we made was putting our trust and loyalty with you."

Leal's face contorts with rage, and he struggles against the ties that are binding him to the chair. "This isn't how this works!" he shouts. "Punishment is to be voted on and declared by the president. Not to mention it should be carried out within the club."

"You're half right. The president does need to declare the punishment after it's put to a vote. You can rest assured that we're following the rules."

"How can you follow the rules when I'm bei—"

"Donovan's our new president," a voice I don't recognize interrupts.

Under the blood on Leal's face, his skin pales. It seems to finally be sinking in that this is a mess he can't get out of, a mess he created for himself. Not only that, but the one person who he might normally get support from gave me her blessing before I walked in this room. He's fucked nine ways to hell, and it's time he accepts that.

"Leonard 'Leal' Alverez, you are hereby stripped of your title as President of the Black Savages. Furthermore, you are stripped of your club patch and of any privileges that you had that can be attributed to the Black Savages. You are no longer welcome on Black Savages' property and we are taking possession of your Harley as payment for damages caused by you."

"You can't do this! I'll make you pay, just you wait and—"

"Oh, did I give you the impression that I was done?" Donovan taunts. "As a result of a vote put to all patched members of the Black Savages MC: Oregon Chapter, which was unanimous by the way, you are sentenced to death at the hands of the Soulless Kings MC: Oregon Chapter."

Leal sputters but doesn't manage to form a coherent sentence in his outrage. The corners of my lips tilt up into a grin, and I know that he sees the beast standing before him. It's not a part of me that I like to unleash, but for him, I'm making an exception.

"Anything else?" I ask Donovan when I turn the screen back around so I can see him.

"Just send us his patch when you're done." The look on Donovan's face is a mixture of resignation, disgust, and determination.

"Sure thing. Now if you'll excuse me, I've got some work to do."

My thumb hovers over the 'end call' button when Donovan stops me.

"And Fender?"

"Yeah?"

"Make him suffer."

Donovan ends the call before I have a chance to. When the screen goes black, I begin to slide it back in my pocket but think better of it at the last second. This isn't going to be a quick killing, and I don't need my phone to get broken in the process.

With Leal's furious pleas ringing in my ears, I turn and walk to the panel by the door and open it to reveal the different buttons. I press the blue one that allows me to see just beyond the door. Charlie's face fills the tiny screen, and there are tears silently falling down her cheeks. I know this is hard for her, and it's about to get worse. No reason for her to stay and watch.

"Charlie, why don't you go see Margo about getting something to eat?"

My voice startles her, and her gaze darts around the hallway looking for the source. Her eyes narrow when she spots the camera and speaker and her lips move.

"Push the button to the right of the door for the intercom," I instruct.

"I'm not hungry," she huffs.

"Babe, please," I plead. I need to do this and the last thing I need is to worry about what she's thinking or feeling as she watches.

"Fender, you promised you'd make it quick."

She might not remember the conversation, but the only actual promise I made was to try to make it quick. "No, Charlie, I didn't." Her face scrunches up as if she's searching her mind for the words that were spoken, words she thinks she'll be able to prove me wrong with.

"Shit," she mumbles when she realizes that I'm right.

"I fucking need you to go, Charlie," I grate out through clenched teeth. "Either you go, or I'm going to have to do this in the dark." That wouldn't be my first choice, turning the lights off so she can't see, but I will if she refuses to walk away.

She tips her head back to look directly at the camera. My heart squeezes at the indecision on her face. It's never easy to choose between family and the person you love, and no one should ever have to. Unfortunately, in our world, that's almost always going to be an issue unless you fall in love with someone inside your own club, with someone who you already call family.

"Fine."

Charlie drops her finger away from the intercom button and crosses her arms over her chest. She doesn't look toward the camera again, just stares at the door for a moment before turning to walk toward the stairs. I watch her go, Leal's screaming behind me for her not to leave him.

I drop my head forward and mumble to myself, "I'm sorry, Charlie. May you and God forgive me."

CHAPTER TWENTY-EIGHT

I've always loved the way my given name rolls off her tongue and right now, in this moment where there's nothing and no one between us, that's who I am.

Fender

"She'll never forgive you for this."

I lift my head slowly as the storm brewing in my soul shifts and gains momentum like a hurricane barreling down on the coastline. Most people would be scared of the power I'm feeling inside, but it only brings me a deadly calm.

"I'm not the one who needs to be worried about her forgiveness," I say, without turning around.

I place my cell on the small shelf inside the panel box and close the metal door. The click of it latching echoes off the walls, and after that, silence. Finally, Leal has shut the fuck up. I pull my gun from my waistband at the small of my back and hold it in front of me. I debate on giving Charlie what she wants: Leal's quick death with a bullet between the eyes.

I dismiss the idea quickly when an image of my father hovering over my mother's lifeless body enters my mind. My body stiffens and the image shifts to Charlie, as a young girl, sleeping on a couch and being photographed without her knowledge. My stomach rolls, and it takes every ounce of control not to throw up. How many other girls did he target? How many other lives has he ruined because he's a sick, twisted fuck?

I shove my gun back in its place and pull out my knife instead. I hold it out in front of me, as if inspecting it, and satisfaction slides through me at Leal's widened eyes. I have to admit, he's put on a great show of being the big, bad biker, but right now, when his life is about to end, he's every bit the pussy it takes to victimize children.

"Ya know," I say, as I run my thumb over the blade. "I think I'm going to enjoy this."

Without waiting for him to say anything, I lunge forward and raise the blade above my head. I swing my arm down and stop just before the tip of the knife sinks into his shoulder. Leal's squirming against his restraints, and I realize that, as much as I want to cause him pain, I also want to make him suffer on a much deeper level.

I switch gears and cut the ties at his wrists and ankles. He stares at me incredulously, and I only give a curt nod. When he stands, his face morphs from scared to cocky confidence. He shakes his arms and legs in what I assume is a way to restore blood flow, but I catch a glimpse of pain across his features at the bullet wound in his knee.

"You shouldn't have done that."

I shrug. "That's where you're wrong. Causing you physical pain isn't my only objective. What better way than to make you hurt, make your soul bleed like mine did, than to beat you when you can fight back? Bringing you down and showing you that you're a worthless piece of shit who never deserved to wear a patch in the first place is the worst I could possibly do, and it's exactly what I'm going to do."

"This isn't exactly a fair fight." Leal nods toward the knife in my hand.

I glance at it and think about his words. He's not wrong so I make a split decision and toss the knife into the corner of the room. Beating him with my bare hands will be so much more satisfying.

"Still got that gun," he says.

I take my gun out and toss it down with the knife.

"Bette—"

His fist slams into my nose, and my head flies back, blood spurting from my nostrils. The cheap shot hurt but only serves to add to my motivation. I force my gaze back to him, and he's standing in a fighter's stance, fists held in front of him, ready to strike.

"Feel better?" I snarl as I swipe at the blood with the back of my hand.

Just as his mouth opens to respond, I pull my knee up and thrust my boot forward to connect with his already busted kneecap. Leal howls in pain and falls to the concrete floor. Maybe this isn't going to be a fair fight after all.

I stand over him, my feet planted on either side of his body. With a look of disgust, I lean down and pick him up by his cut, lifting him off the floor. I haul my arm back and land a blow to his face. I let go with my other hand at the same time, and his head slams into the floor with a sickening crack.

"That was for your brothers."

My fury takes over, and I wail on him with my fists, grunting with each brutal blow. His entire face is swollen and covered in a mixture of his blood and my own. My knuckles are split open, and the pain burns. Sweat beads on my forehead.

"Those were for my parents."

I stand tall and watch as he tries to roll over. My stance doesn't allow him any movement so I lift my right leg and pivot to move to one side. When he's able to get away from me, I let him, and stalk toward my weapons. I pick up my knife and slowly return to stand over him.

"Get up."

Leal moans but doesn't stand.

"Get. The. Fuck. Up."

I bend down and haul him to his feet. He sways but is able to remain upright. I grip his shirt with my left hand and yank him forward, burying the knife in his gut. I leave it there for a minute, my fingers growing slick with his blood as it oozes around the blade.

I lean forward, my mouth close to his ear. "This is for Charlie," I whisper as I jerk the blade upward, slicing open his midsection.

I shove him away from me, and he falls to the floor, landing on his back. The puddle of blood around him grows, but it's still not as big as I'd like. I go back to the corner to retrieve my gun. The weight of it in my hand is familiar, comforting like a mother's hug.

Leal continues to bleed out on the floor, but somehow, he hasn't lost consciousness yet, for which I'm glad. I want him to see me in his last seconds. I want him to enter Hell knowing exactly who sent him there.

I straddle him again and aim the weapon at his head. His eyes are barely open, but they're open enough. I pull the hammer back and bend down, placing the barrel of the gun between his eyes.

"And this, you sick fuck, is for me."

I squeeze the trigger, and the blast fills the room. As I stare at Leal's lifeless body and watch his blood stain the concrete, a sense of peace washes over me. All of the anger, all of the pain, all of the *bad* from the last four years seems to dissipate in a matter of seconds.

I stretch my arm out to grab my knife and grip it as tight as I can so I can remove his patch from his cut. That done, I straighten and allow myself one last kick to my enemy before turning and opening the panel next to the door. I press the button so I can exit. The door slides open, and when I step through, I leave the past behind me so it can be forever discarded with Leal's corpse.

"Holy shit."

Charlie scrambles off the bed and rushes toward me when I enter my room. I'd been scared as hell when I ascended the steps after leaving the Nightmare Room and Charlie was nowhere to be found. Then Piston informed me that she'd gone to my cabin. I handed him Leal's patch and made sure he knew to get it back to the Black Savages and then raced straight here.

"What did he do?"

Charlie's hands roam over my body, trying to find the source of all the blood. I heave a sigh and let myself feel what her touch does to me, let my gaze wander over her exposed flesh.

"Dammit, Fender, where are you hurt?"

Her voice cracks, and my head whips up. She's wearing only a bra and panties and it's hard to focus. I reach out to cup her face, completely ignoring the crimson my touch leaves behind.

"I'm fine, babe. I promise."

"Yeah? You're not exactly the poster boy for promises." I chuckle at her, and she steps back to cross her arms over her chest, her cleavage spilling over the black lace cups trying to hold her in.

"C'mere." When she makes no move to listen, I reach out and lift her wrist toward my mouth. "I know one promise I can make good on now," I whisper just before tracing her infinity tattoo with the tip of my tongue. When she whimpers, I stop, letting her hand fall.

Ignoring her pout, I wrap my arms around her and link my fingers under her ass to lift her up. Her legs go around my waist, and my lips graze hers. I carry her to the bathroom and set her down only long enough for us to strip out of our clothes. After I turn on the shower, I lift her back up and step under the spray.

Red water swirls around the drain, reminding me of what I've just done. I need to wash my sins away before any of it touches her more than it already has. I set her on her feet and grab the soap, but she reaches out to take it from me.

Over the next few minutes, Charlie methodically washes my body and then my hair. With each brush of her hand, each barely there touch of her fingertips, my cock hardens painfully. When the water is finally clear, I bend to pick her up and she stops me, grips my biceps and urges me to switch places with her.

With my back against the wall and the water sluicing over her head, down her body, she kneels in front of me. I know what she's going to do, but even still, I can't stop the sharp intake of breath when her tongue darts out and swirls around my aroused tip.

"Fucking hell," I sputter.

Charlie hums as her lips wrap around my length and she draws me deep. Her nails dig into my ass, and the sting is a stark contrast to what she's doing with my dick. I fist my hands in her hair and tug, just enough that her nails dig deeper.

I let my head fall forward, and my eyes land on my cock sliding in and out of her pink lips. The sight is better than I remember and intensifies the pleasure. I try to pull her off of me, desperately needing to come while inside of her, but she resists and increases her speed.

"Jesus, I'm gonna come," I growl as I give in to the ecstasy.

"Mmmm," she purrs.

My muscles stiffen when her fingers trail from my ass

cheeks to my balls. I throw my head back and let the sensations burn me from the inside out. I shout out my release as my dick pulses in her mouth, and I can feel the suction as she swallows everything I have to give.

When my body relaxes, and I soften on her tongue, she slides her mouth back and stands up with a wide grin. She drags her fingertips up my chest and traces the infinity tattoo before moving her hands to rest on my shoulders. Her slick body aligns with mine and instantly, I'm hard again.

I reach around her to turn the water off and then lift her in my arms so her legs can lock at the small of my back. Stepping out of the shower, I bypass the towels, not giving a damn how wet we are, and carry her into the bedroom. I walk to the bed but detour to the wall before I get there.

I set Charlie on her feet for the time it takes to bend down and shove my arms between her thighs and stand back up with her legs draped over my shoulders and my face buried in her pussy.

"Ah, God," she moans when my tongue connects with her clit.

I smile as I inhale the scent that is uniquely hers. I assault that sensitive bundle of nerves until she tries to buck her hips. I let up on the pressure but continue to mercilessly tease her.

"Fender, I'm… fuck me."

I remove my mouth, and she whines at the loss of contact.

"Hold on, babe."

I carry her to the bed, unable to see a damn thing. When my shins connect with it, I let her fall back onto the mattress, but I don't move my mouth away from her slick center. She reaches out to grab my hair and the moment she tugs, I close my lips around her clit and suck.

Charlie's head thrashes from side to side, and I flatten my hand on her stomach to hold her in place. With my free hand, I penetrate her with two fingers and continue to eat her like a starving man.

"I need..."

"What do you need, Charlie?" I demand when her words trail off.

"You. I need you to fuck me."

Charlie's breathing is ragged, and while a part of me wants to give her what she needs, I don't. Not yet. I continue to slide my fingers in and out of her pussy. Fast, slow, faster, slower. The rhythm of my mouth matches that of my fingers, and when her walls start to clamp down, I increase my pace.

Charlie screams my name as she comes on my tongue, and her arousal coats my hand. When her body relaxes, I push myself up and climb on top of her. Her face is relaxed, and she looks like she could fall asleep any second. Granted, she's satisfied, but I'm not done.

I reach my hand between us and line my dick up with her slit. Charlie's eyes remain closed and her lips in a satisfied smile. Other than the muted moans with each pass of my cock, she's not responding to my touch.

I decide on a different tactic and shift my hand from my dick to her clit and tease her until she's panting, begging again for me to fuck her.

"Still need me?" I ask as I ease my hand away.

"Yes," she hisses.

Unable to hold back any longer, I line myself up and impale her in one smooth stroke. Charlie throws her head back as her spine arches up off the mattress. I lean forward and suck a peaked nipple into my mouth, alternating between forceful sucks and gentle bites.

Charlie undulates her hips, and the frenzy builds as we fuck away all of the demons of our past, only leaving room for the good that's to come. Her nails dig into my back and she hooks her feet behind my thighs, minimizing the space between our bodies, not that there's much to begin with.

I release her nipple and put my mouth to her ear. "You're mine." She nods and I move my hand to her hair and tug. "Say it, Charlie. Say you're mine."

"I-I'm yours," she pants.

"Fucking say my name," I demand as I thrust in and out of her in powerful strokes.

"Fender," she breathes. "I'm yours, Fender."

I pull out of her and flip her over, covering her body with mine and pinning her to the bed. She whines at the loss of contact, and I sit up with my knees on either side of her torso.

"I wanna hear my name come out of your pretty mouth," I demand again, this time with a bite to my tone.

Charlie tries to raise up on all fours, but I'm still too close for her to succeed. I fist my hand in her hair and hold her still until she says what I want to hear.

"Chris!" she shouts. "Fuck, I'm yours, Chris."

I've always loved the way my given name rolls off her tongue, and right now, in this moment where there's nothing and no one between us, that's who I am. Chris, the man who fell in love with her four years ago, the man who loved her even when I hated her, the man who will love her until I draw my last breath.

"On your knees," I command.

Charlie scrambles to her hands and knees, her ass sticking in the air, begging to be smacked. The crack of my palm on her flesh echoes around us, and I rub away the sting before smacking her three more times, each time, soothing the spot that grows red.

I line up my painfully stiff cock and thrust into her so hard that she scoots up the mattress. She braces herself, and I continue to piston in and out of her. Our bodies are sweaty, our moans breathy, raw passion taking over any semblance of rational thought.

Charlie throws her head back and releases a guttural

moan at the same time her pussy spasms. I hold on to her hips as my own fly. My balls tighten, and my spine tingles a split second before my shout matches hers in intensity.

When we both fall back to Earth, I manage to roll to the side as I collapse. We're facing each other, our noses almost touching. She's wearing a satisfied, sleepy smile, and I can't help the grin that forms knowing I'm responsible for it.

"You're mine, too," she murmurs as her eyes slide closed.

"Yeah, Charlotte." I brush a damp strand of hair behind her ear and cup her face. "I'm yours, too."

CHAPTER TWENTY-NINE

My blood will always be Black Savage, but my heart belongs to a Soulless King.

Charlie

A masculine scent with a hint of oil fills my nostrils as I inhale a deep breath. I keep my eyes closed, still not fully awake, but my lips tug into a lazy smile, and I stretch out, prying my arms from the tight embrace I'm wrapped up in.

Fender yawns behind me and lifts his arm off my midsection.

My eyes flutter open, and I roll over to face him.

"Good morning, Chris," I say, tapping his nose and biting my lip to fight my grin.

He chuckles and pulls my hand down to his morning wood. I grip it and smile openly as he hisses.

"That's a name reserved for when I'm fucking you."

"So…" I squeeze again and lean into him to brush my lips over his. "Fuck me."

Fender cups my face and pushes his lips into mine more forcefully than I'm ready for. It takes a moment, but I adjust, and I swirl my tongue with his. It takes no time for my skin to heat and core to tighten.

Fender climbs on top of me and drives into me, and it's only then that I realize how sore I am. My walls protest, but soon I'm able to relax into it. I sink my nails into Fender's shoulders and tug him to me so I can feel the warmth of his chest.

He breathes heavy pants into my ear and thrusts until I come. He pulls out and releases his seed on my leg.

"Fuck, I'm never gonna get tired of that," he says, his hand splayed over his forehead as he rolls over.

I inhale deeply to catch my breath and nod in response. "Me too. Not ever."

"So you're staying then?" He lets his hand drop to the bed and props himself up on his elbows to turn and face me.

He has a satisfied smile from the sex we just had, but there's a hint of worry in his eyes. Like he thinks I actually might go. As if I'm capable.

"Fender." I cup his cheek and shake my head because I can't believe what an idiot he is sometimes. "I love you. I'm not going anywhere ever again."

The sound of a vehicle door slamming reaches my ears, and I whip my head toward the window. When I turn back to Fender, the worry has vanished from his eyes and his smile is wider.

"I'm glad to hear you say that."

He climbs out of bed and starts shuffling through his dresser for clean clothes.

"Who's here?" I ask, pulling the top sheet up to cover my breasts. I sit up and stare out the open doorway.

Fender tosses me some clothes I didn't realize I left here. "Get dressed."

"Fender, what—"

"C'mon," he interrupts, pulling a T-shirt over his head. "Hurry up. We have a big day ahead of us."

I pause another few moments but then start putting on the clothes. Excitement builds with each passing second, and by the time I'm dressed, my smile matches his.

He takes my hand and leads me outside where Piston and Joker are unloading boxes from an SUV onto the front porch. My bike is parked beside it.

"What's all this?" I ask, fingering the cardboard flap on one of the boxes.

Joker steps onto the front porch and gives me a wink. "It's movin' day, darlin'."

"I had them box up your things at your mom's house." Fender says from behind me. I turn to face him and raise a brow.

"But that's not why we have a big day." He steps up to me and runs his hands up and down my arms. Goosebumps spread over my flesh, and my heart pounds with anticipation. "We're going shopping for new furniture and shit." He nods to the house. "Figured since we're gonna to be living together, we should make this your home too."

Warmth spreads from my chest to the rest of my body, and for a moment I just stare.

This guy is such an asshole.

He'll steal me from a mall.

Torture me in a dark room.

Piss all over my heritage and everything I've ever known.

And then he'll make me fall in love with him and want to do it all over again.

I love him. All of him, and I wasn't lying when I said I wouldn't leave. I look over his shoulder in through the living room window and my chest tightens and mouth dries.

This is already my home.

"Is that okay?" Fender asks, tipping my chin up to look at him.

I roll my tongue around to try and get some moisture in my mouth and nod. "Yeah, sounds good."

My voice cracks, but Fender says nothing about it. He bends down and kisses my forehead.

Someone clears their throat behind me.

I spin and face Piston who has a box in his hand and an amused grin. "Do I look like your bitch or somethin'? Give me a hand with this."

I laugh and take the box from Piston, setting it down before walking over to the SUV. The four of us unload the vehicle and leave the boxes on the porch for now.

We start off toward the clubhouse—where apparently Margo makes the absolute best omelets—and leave the SUV behind so Fender and I can take it to go furniture shopping.

I'm laughing at something Joker is saying, and my head is turned, so it hits me by complete surprise when I step through the front door of the clubhouse and am met with a room full of people.

My head snaps forward and my lips part at what I see. Every member of the Soulless Kings, those I've met and some I haven't, is standing around the vast main room with a grin on their faces and a drink in their hand. Hanging on the wall to my right is a homemade sign that reads, "Welcome Home, Charlie".

They lift their glasses and beers and cheer. A few of them yell 'welcome home'.

I don't even have a chance to take it all in and react before I'm swept into the crowd of people and shaking hands with men who days ago wouldn't meet my eyes.

"Squirrel," one of them says, extending a hand with long slender fingers. He's grinning ear to ear at me and reveals a gold crown on one of his teeth. It catches the light and gleams at me.

"Charlie," I say, shaking his hand, although I'm certain we've already met. I understand this, though. This isn't about a first impression or knowing someone's name. This is about acceptance. This is about taking me into their home and declaring me one of theirs. I wonder whose idea this was.

As if compelled by my thoughts, Margo plants a hand on my shoulder and squeezes. I turn to her and let her lead me from the crowd full of damn near drunken bikers even though it's ten in the morning. Apparently, this is a day of celebration.

"You looked a little overwhelmed," she says when we're off to the side of the room. I take a breath and realize it's the first full one since I stepped onto Fender's porch—our porch—and saw boxes of my shit being carried.

"Little bit," I say, still looking around at everyone.

At my new club.

My new *family*.

The thought brings a smile to my face, and I blink to keep from crying. I turn back to Margo. "Thank you for this."

She smiles and throws her arm around me. "Welcome to the family, sweetheart."

My eyes find Fender from across the room. He's talking to Piston, Joker, Greaser and Riker, but he must feel my eyes on him because soon he seeks me out and his gaze lands on me.

Family, I think, staring at the man I love more than anything in this world. I like the sound of that. My blood will always be Black Savage, but my heart belongs to a Soulless King.

I've never felt more at home.

EPILOGUE

They say your life flashes before your eyes the moment just before death. They fucking lied.

Fender

Six months later...

"Mmm, that's one hell of a 'happy birthday'."

Charlie curls into my side and splays her fingers over the tattoo on my chest. I woke up to her mouth on my dick but quickly turned the tables and made her scream my name. A few times, in fact.

"Wait." I roll to my side and let my expression turn concerned. "It's your birthday?"

Her eyes grow wide and for a split second, she looks hurt, but I can't maintain a straight face and when my lips tip up into a grin, she punches me in the arm.

I grab her hand and pull her toward me, laughing as I do.

"Did you really think I wouldn't remember that it's your birthday?"

When she doesn't answer, it's my turn to look hurt. I lean in and press my lips to hers, lightly at first. The kiss is sweet, but my cock quickly hardens and ignites my blood. I thrust my tongue past the seam of her lips and tangle it with hers.

Charlie breaks the kiss and climbs on top of me to straddle my hips. With her hands braced on my pecs, she lowers onto my dick and her velvety heat surrounds me. She throws her head back and rides me and, despite having just gotten off not ten minutes earlier, we both shatter quickly.

"Fuck," I say as a shudder rolls through me. "Whose birthday is it again?"

Charlie chuckles as she scrambles off the bed and struts naked to the bathroom. She throws a sultry look over her shoulder before she crosses the threshold and I rush to join her. We shower together, and as much as I could go for round three, I've got a lot to do before her party this evening and her first surprise is going to be here soon.

As she's putting on the last of her make-up, I stand behind her and admire her reflection in the mirror. Charlie is fucking sexy as hell on her own, but with what she calls her smoky eye look and deep red lipstick, her level of beauty morphs into something that should be illegal.

"You're killing me," I murmur in her ear as I wrap my arms around her waist and nuzzle her neck.

Charlie tilts her head to grant me better access, and a sigh escapes past her slightly parted lips. I nibble her flesh and trace my tongue in lazy circles until my cock strains against my zipper, begging to be freed. I pull away from her on a groan, and my eyes connect with hers in the mirror.

"Maybe I should just stay in my birthday suit today," she says with a saucy grin.

I take a step back and let my gaze drop to her ass, shaking my head. "Nah. I love your ass in these jeans."

"You love my ass no matter what I'm wearing… or not wearing."

"True." I swat her ass. "Hurry up and finish getting ready."

As if on cue, my cell phone rings from the other room, and I hurry to answer it.

"You two managed to get outta bed yet or do I have to come over there and drag you out?"

"Fuck you, Piston," I say, with no heat behind the words.

"Pretty sure your dick couldn't handle it."

"Did you want something?"

"Yeah, Charlie's mom and sister are..."

Charlie steps into the room and Piston's voice fades into the background. I know I just saw her, but my mouth waters at the vision in front of me. Ass-hugging jeans, knee high Harley Davidson boots, tight long-sleeved red tee with a V she cut into it so her cleavage is on display.

"Fender?"

Charlie's hips sway as she saunters over to me.

"Fender?"

Charlie stands in front of me and I can't help but wonder how I got so lucky.

"Fender!"

Piston's voice registers and I shake my head to clear my thoughts.

"What the fuck?" I snap.

"Did you hear a word I said?" Piston asks.

"Ah, yeah." It comes out sounding like a question.

"Good. Should I send them there or what?"

"Who?"

"Jesus, brother." Piston sounds exasperated as hell. "Charlie's mom and sister. Do you want me to send them there or are you guys coming to the clubhouse?"

"Oh, right. Uh, we'll be right there. Keep 'em occupied."

"Fine. But hurry up. It's weird, them being here."

The line goes silent, and it's a full ten seconds before I realize that Piston hung up. I toss the phone on the bed and stand to wrap my arms around Charlie's waist. She extends her arms and holds me at a distance.

"Nope, not happening." She laughs. "I don't know what's going on, but you just said we'd be right there... wherever 'there' is."

"Just grab your cut and let's go."

Charlie looks toward the chair in the corner, where she usually drops her cut at the end of the day.

Rather than wait for me to tell her anything or respond in any way, Charlie struts out of the bedroom. My feet are glued to their spot until I hear the front door open and then I'm running after her. I pull the door shut behind me, the slam bouncing off the trees surrounding our house.

Charlie is already on her bike and revving the engine by the time I straddle mine.

"Follow me," I instruct and she does.

We drive the few minutes to the clubhouse and park our bikes to the right of the porch. I don't see evidence of our visitors, which is good. Piston must've had them park around back.

I guide Charlie inside and to the main room, where her mom and Sylvia are sitting at the bar talking to Margo, looking right at home. They may still be part of the Black Savages family, but they're also a part of mine because they're Charlie's.

Charlie's eyes dart back and forth between me and her family, and then she takes off squealing and launches herself at her sister. As I stand there and watch their interaction, I realize how much Charlie has sacrificed to be with me. She's closer to her mom and Sylvia than she's ever been, according to her, but she doesn't see them as often as she should.

Ever since she moved in with me, Charlie has embraced the Soulless Kings as much as they've embraced her. Things are easier with Leal out of the picture. Fucking prick created a war that didn't need to happen. Soulless Kings and Black Savages will never be friends, but we're no longer sworn enemies. We tolerate each other, and for Charlie's sake, I hope we can keep things that way.

"Looks like you did good."

I turn to see Joker standing there with a beer held out for me. I wrap my fingers around the neck of the bottle and take a long swallow of the cold brew.

"This is just the beginning," I say and my lips tilt into a grin.

∽

The entire Soulless Kings MC: Oregon Chapter is here, and the party is starting to get a little wild. Charlie seems to be having the time of her life, but I've still got a few things up my sleeve and I don't want some dumb drunk fuck to mess them up.

"You better do your thing, man."

Piston slaps a hand on my shoulder, and I glance at him. My heart feels like it's going to beat out of my chest and my palms are sweaty. What the fuck is wrong with me? I'm a badass motherfucker and I don't get nervous. Ever.

Apparently you do.

I walk to the bar and leap up to stand on top of it. Def Leppard is belting through the speakers and I pull my cell out to turn it off. It takes a few seconds, but soon everyone realizes that the music is gone, and they stop dancing.

"Listen up," I shout out over the crowd. "First, I want to thank everyone for coming out to celebrate Charlie's birthday." Cheers fill the air, as do beer bottles and whiskey glasses as everyone salutes Charlie. I turn my attention toward her. "Babe, c'mon up here."

I hold my arm out, inviting her to join me on the bar. She stares at me for a moment, eyes wide, grin wider, before giving in and stretching her arm up. I clasp my hand around her bicep and lift her up to stand next to me.

"Everyone here knows that Charlie and I have a *complicated* story." I pause to let the laughter die down and chuckle as several shouts ring out about how that's an understatement. "But, there's nothing complicated about how I feel about her." I turn to face Charlie, and her face is red with embarrassment. "Charlie, I know you've been riding since the moment your dad gave you your first bike. You grew up with the Black Savages and you've been walking the line between them and the Soulless Kings for a while now."

I lean down to grab the gift-wrapped box that Piston's holding up to me. When I hand it to Charlie, I say, "Happy fucking birthday, babe. I hope you like it."

Charlie wastes no time tearing off the paper and tossing it to the floor. Charlie's always liked presents and I make a mental note to never stop giving her things, even if it's just because. When she lifts the lid and finally glimpses what's inside, her hand flies to her mouth, and her gaze darts back and forth between me and her gift.

"Ya gonna take it out and show everyone or stand there gaping?" Joker yells from the back of the room.

"Shut up, asshole," Charlie quips, although she's laughing as she says it.

When she makes no move to lift her gift out, I do it for her, holding up the leather cut for her and everyone to see. On the back is a Soulless Kings patch with a bottom rocker that reads 'Property of Fender'. On the front left, stitched in red on a white patch are the words 'Black Savage by birth, Soulless King by choice'. On the front right there's a patch with the infinity symbol, that is identical to our matching tattoos.

Charlie snatches the cut out of my hands and looks at each patch with a giant smile on her face.

"Charlie," I start, and she raises her eyes to mine. "I love you so fucking much. I already made you a partner in Infinite Motors, you share my house, my bed, my love of riding and my sense of loyalty." I reach into my pocket, pull out the box that's been burning a hole there all day and get down on one knee. Charlie's hand flies to her mouth. "I know that we don't need a piece of paper to be partners in life and, as far as I'm concerned, you're already my ol' Lady, but how 'bout we make it official? Will you marry me? Be a Soulless King's queen and stand beside me, no matter what, for the rest of our lives?"

Charlie doesn't say anything for a moment, and my stomach starts to drop. I glance at Piston and he shrugs as if to say 'no idea what's going on'. I slowly rise to my feet and the moment I lift my foot to step toward her, she jumps up and wraps her legs around my waist. I stumble backward even as my arms catch her.

"Is that a yes?" someone shouts from the crowd.

"Babe, I kinda want the answer to that question, too."

I try to make light of my nerves, but she's killing me.

"No, it's not a yes," Charlie says, her voice clear and loud.

My arms grow weak and my vision blurs. That is *not* at all what I was expecting. I try to set Charlie on her feet, but she tightens her legs and her arms around my neck.

"It's a fuck yes."

Cheers erupt in the room, and Charlie's lips crash into mine.

They say your life flashes before your eyes the moment just before death. They fucking lied.

Your life flashes before your eyes the moment you realize you have everything that makes life worth living.

BONUS CHAPTER

Need more of Fender and Charlie? Sign up for our newsletters at andirhodes.com and nicolecypher.com for an EXCLUSIVE bonus chapter, as well as updates on upcoming novels and giveaways.

ABOUT ANDI RHODES

Andi Rhodes is an author whose passion is creating romance from chaos in all her books! She writes MC (motorcycle club) romance with a generous helping of suspense and doesn't shy away from the more difficult topics. Her books can be triggering for some so consider yourself warned. Andi also ensures each book ends with the couple getting their HEA! Most importantly, Andi is living her real life HEA with her husband and their boxers.

For access to release info, updates, and exclusive content, be sure to sign up for Andi's newsletter at andirhodes.com.

ABOUT NICOLE CYPHER

Nicole Cypher is an author and avid reader of dark romance. She began her writing journey in college and hasn't looked back since. In her books you can expect a yummy anti-hero, plenty of action, and a happy ending.

Be sure to sign up for her newsletter at nicolecypher.com to stay up to date on the latest releases, special offers, and exclusive bonus chapters.

ALSO BY ANDI RHODES

Broken Rebel Brotherhood

Broken Souls

Broken Innocence

Broken Boundaries

Broken Rebel Brotherhood: Complete Series Box set

Broken Rebel Brotherhood: Next Generation

Broken Hearts

Broken Wings

Broken Mind

Bastards and Badges

Stark Revenge

Slade's Fall

Jett's Guard

Soulless Kings MC

Fender

Joker

Piston

Greaser

Riker

Trainwreck

Squirrel

Gibson

Satan's Legacy MC

Snow's Angel

Toga's Demons

Magic's Torment

ALSO BY NICOLE CYPHER

For a comprehensive list, check out Nicole's website

The Darker Places Series:

DESIRED

DEPLORABLE

DETHRONED

DEMOLISHED

JULIUS

Soulless Kings MC:

FENDER

JOKER

Gruco Crime Family Series:

HIS PROMISE

HIS PET

HIS PRIZE

HIS PUPPET

HIS PROPERTY

Standalone Novels:

UNHINGED

VICIOUS KNIGHT